COWBOY PROUD

KINGS OF MONTANA, BOOK 4

VANESSA GRAY BARTAL

DRY CREEK PRESS

CHAPTER 1

*J*osh King felt completely grown up. At eighteen he was the youngest of the four King brothers. Not that you would know it by their behavior lately. All three of them were *in love.* As far as Josh could tell being in love meant your brain turned to mush and all rational thought flew out the window.

Take his brother Cameron, for instance. His old friend, Belle, came back into town after a four-year absence and suddenly his most sensible brother was jumping into the spring in the middle of the night to have a breath-holding contest with the woman who looked too fancy to have ever lived in their small town. Then, to make matters worse, he went to New York with Belle for what was supposed to be a short weekend and came home three weeks later married. Not only that, but he announced he would be living half the year in New York. New York, the place that, as far as Josh was concerned, was the center of all debauchery.

And then there was Coy, although his idiocy didn't really surprise Josh. Coy had always been the most flighty and, perversely, the most well liked brother. No one had been too surprised when he married Cam's girlfriend, Ivy, only four weeks after having met her, least of all Josh.

Surprisingly, Cade had been the only one to do things properly, the way they should be done. Once upon a time Cade had been the brother Josh agreed with the least. He was fun like Coy, only with a more stubborn will that seemed dead set about getting into trouble. Then he was stepped on by a bull and became paralyzed from the waist down. Maybe the accident had some type of maturing effect on him. Whatever the reason, Cade had met his Layla and taken time building up to an engagement—almost two years. They were planning a proper wedding and everyone in town would be invited, exactly as it should be.

Josh knew when the time came for him to find a girl and settle down, he would do things the right way. He would take his time courting her, they would have a long engagement, and then they would be married in the town where they would spend the rest of their lives. No quickie, cagey elopements for him, although he had learned the hard way to keep his feelings to himself. Whenever he tried to inform his brothers of his plans, they simply laughed at him. If there was one thing Josh couldn't stand, it was to be ridiculed.

But now, as he sped toward his destination in Wyoming, he tried to put thoughts of his brothers out of his mind. After all, it was because they were all so besotted that he had been allowed to take the cattle to Wyoming alone—a first, and a sign of their trust in him. Not that he was actually alone, he reminded himself. But their cowhand, Sam, was so comfortable to be around Josh almost forgot about him.

There were some people with whom silence was uncomfortable. Some of their hands were chatty, always feeling the need to fill silence with their own voices. But Sam wasn't one of those. He was the strong silent type, and Josh appreciated that characteristic more than any other. Though, if he were being honest, he would admit there was a lot about Sam he appreciated. He was intelligent, hard working, and loyal. True, he was small for a cowboy, but their old hand Shorty was small and wiry, too. Size didn't always matter. Sam was a hard worker, and that was what counted most.

Josh felt vindicated by Sam's work ethic. In the beginning, Cam hadn't wanted to hire Sam. It had been he, Josh, who took one look at the potential employee, saw something he liked, and stepped in to change Cam's mind. And since Josh usually left all employment decisions up to his brother, Cam had been surprised enough to listen. Sam, thankfully, had seemed bent on proving his worth, which he had done many times over. He was always the first one in the saddle in the morning, and the last one to leave. Unlike the other hands who enjoyed their leisure time off the clock, Sam could often be found around the barn looking for extra work. Sometimes he simply brushed the horses for something to do, as if he couldn't *not* be doing something.

Over the course of Sam's employment the last six months, he and Josh had become a team. Wherever Josh was, there was Sam. Some of the others were beginning to tease Josh about his shadow, but he didn't mind. Sam was grateful Josh had stuck up for him, that was all. Josh understood and appreciated that sort of loyalty. As an added bonus, he genuinely liked Sam. He was intelligent, well spoken, and well-mannered. He was a bit shy with the other cowboys, but that was a fair trade for someone who arrived at work early and lacking a disgusting trail of tobacco juice on his chin, as some of their more seasoned cowboys were apt to do. In the beginning, he had been shy around Josh, too, but after so much time spent working together he had come out of his shell and now talked freely, though only when he actually had something to say—another plus, in Josh's opinion.

When Cam informed him that he, Josh, was going to be the one making the Wyoming run today, it had been a no-brainer that Sam would be the one to go with him. Although, in retrospect, Sam had been less than thrilled by the prospect when Josh first mentioned it to him.

"Don't you want to go to Wyoming?" Josh had asked, exasperated. It was a cake job, basically a day off from the saddle that anyone would give their right arm for. No doubt Josh was creating resentment by choosing their newest employee for the honor.

"Course I do," Sam had said. "I don't like staying in hotels, is all. I don't share a bed with another man." He had crossed his arms defiantly over his chest.

Josh had rolled his eyes. "Who does? Of course we're getting two beds. Don't be stupid. I'd rather sleep on the floor than share a bed with you."

"So would I," Sam said, and that had been the end of the argument.

Now Sam sat quietly absorbed in a paper he bought when they stopped to fill up the truck.

"What are you reading about?" Josh asked.

"Political unrest in Ethiopia," Sam replied.

Josh wasn't surprised by the response. Sam was interested in world events, something that had never much concerned Josh. He had his little corner of the world, and that was enough. Still, he was interested enough to listen when Sam talked about world politics, which he did often as they rode fences or did any of the other menial tasks that would otherwise be boring without conversation.

"Why don't you go to college?" Josh blurted suddenly. He had no plans to attend college, but then he didn't need to. He owned a ranch and had received on-the-job training from birth. Most of their help enjoyed working with their hands and couldn't be described as thinkers, but Sam was different. Josh had noticed from the first that Sam was more refined and intelligent than most of the cowboys they employed, especially the transient loners. Most drifters had a past they were hiding from, usually criminal. But at eighteen, Sam was too young to be running from a felony.

"Maybe I will," Sam replied, grinning. "As soon as my boss starts paying me enough to cover tuition. I've got my eye on Harvard." He rattled his paper and returned to reading.

Josh snorted a laugh, trying to picture Sam in his cowboy boots and Stetson attending Harvard. His laugh died when he realized the picture wasn't all that unlikely. Somehow Sam would fit in among the rich and elite. It was odd. Maybe he was a runaway from somewhere wealthy. Maybe that explained his cultured, reserved way of speaking.

"Is your family rich?" Josh asked.

Sam's fingers tensed on the paper. "No, I told you. My mom died a few years ago, and my step dad was with the rodeo."

Sam had told him, making sure to include the fact that his stepfather wasn't a performer with the rodeo, but simply a roadie who helped with the equipment and animals. The animosity in his voice had told Josh there was no love lost between the two men.

They finished the trip to the stockyard without incident, conversing occasionally when the mood struck. They were the last delivery of the day for the yard, and Josh could tell everyone was ready to go home. He and Sam hopped from the truck and opened the gate while their cows shuffled out.

"Did you see that cow look at me?" Sam said when they finished their task and returned to the truck. "It was like he knew why I brought him here."

Josh laughed. Sam was the first hand he had met who seemed to have fits of conscience over the ultimate end their cows met. Or at least he pretended to in order to entertain Josh. Sometimes he took it so far as to make up narratives for the cows, such as escape plots they were brewing in order to evade their fate.

Last month Josh had almost fallen off his horse with laughter when Sam detailed for him the latest plot he was sure the cows had hatched. As they sat on their horses watching the herd, Sam had done different voices for the cows, acting out their conversation. It was something a bored cowboy might do in his head but didn't usually share with others. With good reason, too. While Josh might understand that Sam was different, the others wouldn't. Thankfully Sam was too reticent to say much around anyone else, and therefore Josh was the only one who was included in his odd displays of humor. Not that he was complaining. Sam was strange, but he was funny. Despite the fact that Josh had three brothers who were all close in age, he thought maybe Sam was the best friend he ever had. Somehow Sam seemed to get him in a way his brothers never had.

Since they had nothing to do for the rest of the evening in a strange town, they decided to skip fast food and eat a leisurely dinner at a sit-down restaurant.

"So, I decided to ask Chelsea out," Josh inserted casually into conversation as soon as they placed their order.

"Hmm," was Sam's reply. He stared at his plate, studiously arranging his place setting.

Josh sighed. What had he been hoping for, a high five? Though Sam had never come out and said anything against the girl Josh had had a crush on for much of his life, he made no secret of his distaste for her.

"I don't know why you don't like her," Josh said irritably.

"I didn't say a word," Sam said. "She's not my type, but that doesn't mean she can't be yours." Despite his words, Josh still sensed his disapproval, and it made him angry. He had never asked a girl out before, choosing instead to bide his time and make sure she was the one he wanted. But there were other forces involved now. They were eighteen, and Chelsea was too good to be on the market for long. Already she had dated Chad Parker. They broke up a couple of weeks ago, and Josh felt pressured to make a move before anyone else did.

"Who is your type?" Josh asked. "I've never heard you mention a girl. Is there someone from back home?"

"No, there's no one from back home," Sam said. "I'm not ready to date yet."

Josh nodded. "That's sensible. Take your time until you're ready."

"Although now that Chelsea is back on the market, maybe I'm ready now," Sam said.

Even though Josh knew he was teasing, there was still a part of him that felt a desperate need to call Chelsea and ask her out right now. Not that Chelsea would go out with Sam anyway. On the few occasions they had met, the feeling of dislike seemed to be mutual.

"If you had asked her to dance on Founder's Day, maybe you would actually have a shot," Josh said. While he had danced with a handful of girls at their town's annual celebration, he hadn't been able to coax Sam into talking to a girl, much less ask one to dance.

"She's taller than me," Sam said sullenly, which had also been his excuse the night of the dance.

"Who isn't?" Josh asked.

Sam frowned at him, but their food arrived before he could make a reply.

After supper Josh suggested they see a movie. Since the town was much larger than theirs, it had a multiplex with ten cinemas, an almost overwhelming number of choices for Josh.

"You choose," Josh said, suddenly feeling ready to get back to their tiny town where everything was as it should be.

"That one." Sam pointed to an action flick and Josh slumped in relief. After telling Sam to choose, he immediately feared Sam might choose something cerebral with subtitles.

They watched the movie in silence and went back to their hotel. It was early, but there was nothing to do besides watch television. Since the next day was going to include twelve hours of driving, and since they had been driving since four that morning, they decided to turn in early.

Josh showered and clicked on the television to watch while Sam took his turn in the bathroom. The blare of the television did nothing to cover the click of the bathroom lock, however. Josh looked at the door and shook his head with a laugh. As if he would walk in on Sam in the shower. Sometimes that kid was a little too reserved. He was one of only a handful of employees who chose to live in town rather than sleep in the bunkhouse. He could have had more pocket money or savings or whatever without having to pay rent, but it was really none of Josh's business. Privacy was apparently important to Sam, which was one more thing that made him different, but not necessarily bad.

He was half asleep when Sam exited the shower, but he was awake enough to notice the flannel pajama pants and long-sleeved shirt he wore. Since it was June and warm outside, Josh was sleeping in his usual boxer shorts.

"Where's your parka?" Josh asked.

"I get cold when I sleep," Sam replied. "It's because I don't have much body fat, unlike some people."

"You're one weird little cowboy," Josh said sleepily before turning out the light and falling asleep.

CHAPTER 2

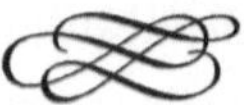

The next morning, Sam repeated his routine of locking the bathroom door while he was getting ready. Josh had the sudden temptation to break into the room and yell "aha!" to scare him. But since he had no real desire to break in on another man while he was in the bathroom, he let the thought go.

Josh took his turn and they went to eat breakfast before starting the long journey home. They ate at a truck stop located adjacent to a convenience store. As was his custom, Josh ordered the full breakfast with eggs, bacon, hash browns, toast, biscuits, gravy, orange juice, and coffee. Sam ordered coffee and a fruit cup.

"A fruit cup?" Josh said disdainfully.

"I'm not that hungry in the mornings," Sam said. He turned his attention to the newspaper in front of him.

"You're never hungry," Josh said disgustedly. "Sam, you've got to start acting like a cowboy if you want to be taken seriously on the ranch. You have to stop reading every time you get a break, start eating enough to put some muscle on your bones, stop feeling sorry for the animals, and start asking some girls out. The other men are starting to talk, and there's only so long I can run interference for you."

Sam set aside his paper and picked up his coffee to take a sip before folding his hands around the mug. "I appreciate what you're trying to do here, Josh, but I'm never going to fit into the mold you're trying to create for me. I'm never going to be anybody's idea of a cowboy."

"Then why stay in this life?"

"Because it's all I know. The man my mother married dragged me all over with the rodeo. I hated the traveling, hated being out of school, so I made do with whatever books I could get my hands on. And I learned how to care for the animals. It was the only thing I seemed to be any good at."

Sam was a natural with the animals, both cows and horses. He had a natural affinity that worked to calm them when he was in their presence. "Then why not do what I suggested?" Josh said. "Why not go to college and learn to do something else?"

"I can't afford to go to college," Sam said placidly. "I'm trying to save up, but I never seem to get very far."

Josh was reaching the end of his patience. "Then move out to the ranch. The bunkhouse is provided as part of your salary. You could save that much more if you didn't have to pay rent every month" Plus maybe if he lived with the other hands, they would develop more of a bond with him and stop making fun of him so much for being different.

"I like my privacy," Sam said placidly.

"You're being stubborn," Josh accused.

Sam grinned. "A trait we have in common."

Josh rolled his eyes. "Finish your fruit so we can get on the road."

"Sure thing, Boss," Sam muttered, polishing off his fruit far before Josh was finished with his monstrous meal.

Josh paid for their food and decided to take a coffee to go. He would need all the caffeine he could get because he planned on driving the entire twelve hours. They had used a semi to deliver the cows, and Sam didn't have his commercial driver's license. Plus Josh had a hard time imagining the little guy handling a big rig. Now he tossed Sam the keys so he could unlock the truck and wait inside while Josh waited in line to pay for his coffee.

He stared absently at the parking lot as Sam walked toward the truck. His steps were bouncy light and not at all appropriate for a cowboy who wanted to be taken seriously.

"Sam, Sam, Sam," Josh mumbled under his breath. "What am I going to do with you?"

When it was Josh's turn in line, he took a step forward and froze, his mouth twisted in horror. "No," he said, but it was too late. A car came barreling around the corner of the convenience store, oblivious to the man in its path. There was no time to react or shout a warning. Sam didn't even have time to try and jump out of the way before the car barreled into him, throwing him a couple of feet into the air before he landed on the car's hood. The car slammed on its brakes and Sam rolled onto the ground.

Josh ran from the restaurant, and only after he reached Sam did he realize he was holding his coffee. He tossed it in a trashcan before kneeling beside his friend. To his relief, Sam was conscious, although he was confused. He kept trying to get up. Josh laid a hand on his shoulder and pushed him back down.

"Sam, lie still until the ambulance arrives." He looked around, suddenly realizing an ambulance might not be coming. "Did anyone call 911?"

"I did," the cashier answered from somewhere to Josh's left side. "They want to know his condition. I'll go back and tell them." She turned and ran back inside.

"I don't want to go to the hospital," Sam said. His protest might have been more believable if his eyes stopped rolling back in his head every few seconds.

"It's okay," Josh said comfortingly. "You're on ranch business. The ranch will pay for your care."

"No. Can't go to hospital. Promise, Josh, promise won't let them take me to…hospital."

"I'm not promising that, Sam. Lie back and close your eyes. I can hear the sirens."

Either Sam did as directed or he passed out, giving Josh the opportunity to turn angry eyes on the person who had hit his friend. Then, seeing a frail old woman who was practically hysterical over what she'd done, his anger deflated. Thankfully someone else from the store was tending to her because she looked like she would soon be in need of medical attention if she became any more upset.

The ambulance arrived and began firing off questions at Josh while they loaded Sam.

"How old is he?" the driver asked.

"Eighteen," Josh answered.

"Does he have any allergies?"

"I don't think so," Josh said.

"Does he have diabetes, history of heart disease, epilepsy, brain disorders?"

"I don't know. He's never mentioned any of those things," Josh said. For the first time this trip he felt very young. Sam was in his care, and he knew too little about him to properly take care of him. He stood aside and watched helplessly while Sam was loaded into the ambulance and driven away, lights and sirens blaring.

"Where is the hospital?" Josh asked the bystander who had helped the old woman. She gave him detailed directions he didn't bother writing down. Hospitals were usually well marked. The only problem would be trying to wind a semi through crowded city streets.

Thankfully the hospital ended up being on a main thoroughfare. That left only the problem of trying to find parking. He eventually parked at the far back of the lot, taking up six spaces. Since there were still so many spots open nearby, he didn't think it was a problem.

The walk to the emergency room took forever. He would need to call Cam and alert him of the accident, but for now his main concern was checking on Sam. Josh felt bile rising in the back of his throat. How could the little guy be okay after taking a hit like that? What if he died?

No, he wouldn't think that way. Sam had been conscious when Josh reached him. He would hold onto that thought as the beacon of hope it was. Sam had been alive when he left in the ambulance. There was no reason to believe that would have changed.

He forced himself to wait in line at the emergency room calmly and patiently. When he reached the front desk, he spoke clearly, betraying no hint of his inner emotional turmoil.

"My friend was brought in by ambulance a little while ago. He was hit by a car."

"Name?" the woman said, her business-like tone betraying the fact that, to her, being hit by a car was a mundane occurrence.

"Sam McCoy," Josh said.

The woman looked at her computer before turning to sift through a stack of clipboards behind her. "He's still being processed," she said after a minute of searching. "We'll call you when the doctor is ready to speak to you." She looked behind him, effectively stopping his questions before he could ask them. "Next," she called.

Josh shuffled out of the way and sat down. A magazine was lying face up on the table in front of him. The headline blared something about the political unrest in Ethiopia. Josh laughed, but his voice broke embarrassingly, choking him into silence. What was wrong with him? As a lifelong rancher, he was no stranger to injuries; he had seen plenty of cowboys bleeding and bruised.

Although he had never seen any of them hit by a car. None of them were as small and helpless-looking as Sam. And none of them had meant quite as much to him as Sam did. Though they had only known each other six months, Sam now meant as much to him as any of his brothers. Maybe more so because Josh had set himself up as Sam's protector. He couldn't imagine losing him.

After what seemed like forever, a nurse called his name. He dashed to his feet, wringing his Stetson nervously between his fingers.

"You're the man who came in with the car accident?" the doctor said.

"Yes," Josh replied. The doctor's expression and tone were neutral, betraying nothing of Sam's condition.

"Your friend is going to be all right," the doctor said.

Josh relaxed so much his shoulders sagged and he shuffled forward.

"Amazingly, there are no broken bones and no internal injuries. There is a concussion and some bruising of the thigh bone. A bone bruise is as painful as a break and takes longer to recover, but, once recovered, there should be no lingering effects."

Could Sam really have gotten off so easily after such a horrific accident? Maybe the old woman hadn't been going as fast as it seemed. Maybe she hadn't hit Sam as hard as it looked from inside the store.

"Are you sure?" Josh asked.

The doctor nodded. "I'm positive. I checked her very thoroughly."

Josh's relief was short-lived. "I think we must not be talking about the same person. I'm here for one of my ranch hands. He's about so big." He held up his hand to his chest. "Dark hair, blue eyes. He was dressed like me." He looked down to indicate his jeans and plaid shirt.

The doctor nodded. "Yes, I know who you're talking about. We only have one car accident victim right now. Sam McCoy, right?"

Now it was Josh's turn to nod. "But Sam's a boy."

The doctor grinned. "Son, after four years of medical school and two dozen more in practice, I'm pretty sure I know what a girl looks like." Though he was clearly amused by the situation, he didn't stick around to indulge his amusement. Instead he turned on his heel and went back into the restricted area after telling Josh he could visit "her" whenever he wanted.

But Josh remained staring at the swinging door, dumbstruck. What was the doctor talking about? Of course there was some mistake. His heart started to beat hard, and his palms started to sweat. Had they overlooked Sam somehow or gotten him mixed up with someone else? Obviously so, or how else to explain things?

As he started to walk through the double set of swinging doors, he found that his legs felt rubbery. Once again he was consumed by the fear that Sam might have died. How else could such a dire mix up have occurred?

So preoccupied was he by these confusing thoughts that it took several wrong turns and a stop at the nurses' station before he finally found Sam's room.

And when he stepped into the room, he knew.

Sam was sitting up facing the window, and doing nothing to stop the flow of tears streaming down his cheeks. *Her* cheeks, Josh amended himself. He stopped short in the doorway. Sam turned stricken eyes on him, guilt and fear lining her features. Even now, as confused and angry as he was, the sight of Sam in pain brought an echoing twist in Josh's heart. But he easily ignored it.

"Josh, please, I," Sam started, but Josh didn't let her explain. Instead, he turned and walked from the room. He didn't stop walking until he reached his truck, and then he drove all the way home.

CHAPTER 3

wo Years Later...

"Josh, do you want to go to the store with me?"

Josh removed the two-way radio from his hip and pressed the button to talk to his sister-in-law, Layla. "Sure. When are you leaving?"

"As soon as possible. Do you need to shower first?"

He smiled at the radio. "Nah, I've been on light duty today. See you in a few." He had been trying in vain to repair one of Ivy's fancy saddles. Though everyone had told him a professional would have to do it, Josh was stubbornly convinced he could mend it himself and avoid the expensive repair. Now he tossed the saddle onto its wall hook in frustration. He hated failing, but, even more, he hated being proved wrong. At least he had the comfort that his brothers seemed to be maturing past the point where they teased him every time it happened.

When he was little, they had nicknamed him "Saint Josh" and gloried over any fault they found in him, real or perceived. But nowadays since they had all married, they had mellowed in their treatment of him. He couldn't help but believe his sisters-in-law were responsible. None of them could stand to see him teased, especially not Ivy who had five older brothers of her own. He would never admit to anyone that he enjoyed the slight coddling his sisters-in-law gave him. Their deference to his status as the youngest was a soothing balm after being at the mercy of his brothers' teasing for so many years.

Still, it could have been worse. He could have been the youngest in *Ivy's* family. He shuddered, thinking of the five brothers who had made an annual visit each of the last three years to check on their sister. The last time, the county sheriff had politely suggested that if they ever came back they shouldn't leave the ranch. Not that they had done anything illegal, or even immoral. But their boisterous pranks had left the town in an uproar. Rumor had it that some of the town's residents were still wearing someone else's underwear because of what had been an elaborate panty swap by the brothers. No one was even sure how they had pulled off what they had done, but everyone had a whole lot of sympathy for Ivy who had endured twenty two years of their "humor."

"Did you get it fixed?" Ivy asked as she passed him on her way into the barn.

"No," Josh said.

"Oh, well thanks for trying, Josh." She gave him a sweet smile before returning her mind to business.

Josh had a smile of his own as he headed toward the house. Leave it to Ivy to chalk up his stubborn refusal to admit failure as some type of favor to her. He liked all of his brothers' wives and, after some of his friends' siblings had married, he realized what a rare thing that was. He even liked Belle, though their relationship had taken a long time to develop. Not only had Josh blamed her for leading his brother to New York for half the year, but she had seemed too cool and sophisticated to blend in with their family.

Then, slowly, they had both lowered their guards enough to get to know each other and Josh realized that, despite her outward appearance, she was a small town girl at heart, if a bit more clumsy than most. In fact, the first thaw in their relationship came when Josh rescued her from the pigpen. To this day, he had no idea how she wound up in there or why the ten baby pigs were chasing her around their pen, squealing angrily.

And then there was Layla. If he had to choose a favorite among the three females, it would be Layla, but maybe that was because, at four years, she had been with them the longest. Or maybe it was because she had no family, save them. Or maybe it was because she used to be their housekeeper and had set herself up as his caretaker, making sure he was well fed and clothed. Whatever the reason, she felt most like a sister to him, and he could talk comfortably with her about any issue. Any issue but one, he amended, pushing the matter from his mind before his usual anger could rise to the surface again.

"That was fast," she said now. "Do you want to drive?"

"What do you think?" he asked.

She smiled and tossed him the keys to the truck. "I think Montana has made you predictable. It wouldn't kill you to let a girl chauffer you around sometime."

"It might, and that's a chance I'm not willing to take," he said. He opened the passenger door for her and held out a hand to help her inside. He was big on observing all the rules of polite society. Some people thought that made him old fashioned. He preferred to think of it as chivalry.

"What are you going to town for?" he asked.

"This and that," she replied vaguely. "What about you?" She smiled knowingly at him.

"This and that," he replied. In truth, they both knew he was going to visit his girlfriend. While he had never cared much for town before, it held a whole new fascination for him the last few months he and Chelsea had been dating.

Layla studied her youngest brother-in-law with a smile. He smiled in return, causing both his deep dimples to flash. Besides growing taller and filling out some, she didn't think he had aged one minute since she first laid eyes on him four years ago. His face remained boyish and sweet, which was a sharp contrast to his serious nature. She had wondered if age and maturity would work to mellow him, but so far that hadn't happened. He was still dogmatic in his convictions and unforgiving to anyone who crossed him, something that worried his family more than a little. The men of the family had tried to tease him out of his somber state, but the women pointed out that they were only alienating him. Since then, they had all tried the women's approach of loving him out of his grave moods.

No doubt Josh would curl up and die if he knew he had been the topic of several family meetings over the last couple of years, but he had. They were all worried about him and concerned his stern unrelenting nature was going to lead to more trouble than it already had. Thankfully they felt they were starting to see some signs of softness since he started dating Chelsea. Even though the family didn't much care for the girl, they were willing to give her a pass if she was able to reach Josh's frozen heart. That was why each of them took him to town with them at every opportunity. If something was working to soften Josh, then they would do whatever they could to nudge it along.

"You can drop me here," Layla said when they reached the edge of town.

Josh looked at her in question. "Why would I drop you here? There's nothing nearby."

"I'll walk from here. It's no big deal. I know you're anxious to get to Chelsea."

He frowned. "Layla, don't be silly. I'll take you where you want to go."

She bit her lip. "I need to go to the drugstore, Josh."

His expression turned thunderous, his hands clenched on the steering wheel and his brow pulled low over his eyes. All traces of his dimples were gone.

Resolutely, he faced forward and gunned the accelerator.

"Josh, you don't have to do this. I'm capable of walking."

He remained silent until they reached the parking lot, then he stopped the truck and shifted into park before turning to Layla. When she saw his angry expression, she shrank back and reached for the door.

"I don't need you or anyone else to protect me. I'm not a child. I can come and go to the drugstore whenever I please. What time do you want picked up?"

"An hour," she said, trying not to let the hurt register in her tone. Josh was Josh. Most likely he had no idea the effect he had on people when he was so harsh.

He nodded curtly and faced forward again while Layla descended the truck. The fact that he didn't offer her assistance was a sign of how angry he was; he was usually fastidious about manners, especially where a woman was concerned. Gently, she closed the door and turned to face the store. She wondered if he would still be angry when he showed up again. Usually, he afforded more grace and forgiveness toward his family, but if something didn't work soon to change him from his hardened mold, there was no telling how he would end up. His brothers only had so much patience for him. If Cade had heard Josh talking to his wife that way, the resulting scene wouldn't have been pretty.

But he hadn't heard, and Layla certainly wasn't going to tell him. She could only hope and pray something would happen to soften Josh's heart, the sooner, the better.

With that thought in mind, she entered the drugstore and separated a shopping cart from the line of carts in the entryway. Since she so rarely got to town, her list was massive. For a while when she was first starting her business, she had been too busy to take time off, even to see to her family's needs. Cade had done all the shopping for her, which resulted in some interesting choices when she sent him to the store for makeup or feminine hygiene products. She, Ivy, and Belle had spent a long time laughing over the garish, almost fluorescent pink blush he had bought because he had thought it would look better on her than her usual color. Then when she modeled it for him, he had laughed, too, promising never to stray from her list again.

Since she sold her candy business to a company in Oregon a few months ago, she had too much time on her hands. Going to the drugstore was a reasonable way of filling that time and she planned to stroll the aisles leisurely, enjoying having a purpose again, even if it was only for an hour.

The hour sped by and Layla reluctantly made her way to the checkout aisle. Not only did she not want to interrupt the fun of shopping, but she wasn't looking forward to facing Josh on the long ride back to the ranch. She could only hope that his time visiting Chelsea would work to sooth his ruffled feelings.

"Hi, Layla."

The soft, gentle voice startled Layla out of her reverie, forcing her to smile at the speaker. "Hi, Sam."

Sam returned her smile before dropping her eyes to the register and beginning to scan Layla's items. Layla studied her as she did so. There was such a lost lamb quality about the girl; she engendered a protective feeling in Layla and almost everyone else who encountered her. The town had adopted her as one of their own and everyone looked out for her. As Layla studied her now, she wondered how any of them had ever mistaken her for a boy. Of course her hair had been short two years ago where now it hung to her shoulders. And she had seemingly bound her breasts because she had a pleasant, if petite, figure now. But beyond those two things, she was so fragile-looking and feminine it was a wonder any of them had been taken in by the ruse. Her features were delicate, except her eyes which were dark blue and almost too large for her elfin face. The fact that her face was heart-shaped did nothing to hide the illusion of her too-large eyes. They seemed to pop over her tipped up nose and pointed chin.

"How are you, Sam?" She asked the question every time she came into the drugstore, and every time Sam answered the same way.

"I'm fine, thank you for asking. And how are you?"

"I'm doing well."

That was usually the extent of their exchange, but today Sam continued. "And how is…how are things at the ranch?" She looked up from the scanner and pinned Layla with eyes that spoke volumes.

Layla blinked against the sudden sting of tears as she read unfathomable pain in the other girl's eyes. "Things are good," Layla said, her voice choked. *If you're asking if he's forgiven you, the answer is no.*

Sam blinked twice before returning her attention to her duty.

"Are you ready?"

They both froze as Josh spoke from behind Layla. Sam's hand gripped the box of toothpaste so tightly she was in danger of crushing it.

"Almost," Layla said, striving for a casual tone. She hoped her words would goad Sam back into action, and they did. Sam continued scanning, concentrating very hard now so she wouldn't mess up or reveal her shaking hands.

She announced the total to Layla and stood still while Layla fished out her credit card and paid. She remained silent while she ripped the receipt from the register and shoved it in one of the bags. But then she couldn't take it anymore and, despite her better judgment, she spoke.

"Hi, Josh," she said in a shy whisper.

Giving no indication anyone had spoken, Josh collected Layla's bags, turned, and stormed from the store.

CHAPTER 4

Samantha McCoy finished her day on autopilot. After so many years of suppressing her emotions, she was almost a pro at it. She even managed to make small talk and smile with a few of the customers who showed up after Layla.

When work was finished, she walked slowly back to her tiny apartment behind the feed mill and let herself in. One of the many things she liked about this town was that she never had to lock her door while she was away. At night when she slept, she always secured it because a girl alone couldn't be too careful. But during the day, anyone was free to come in and steal her hotplate, chair, or single mattress on the floor. No one ever did, and she preferred to think it was because the town was trustworthy and not because her possessions were so shabby that not even criminals wanted them.

She opened the lone cupboard and took out a plastic container that housed her saltine crackers. Breaking a cracker in half, she set it on the floor before sitting on her mattress to wait. He didn't keep her waiting long; soon a little mouse scurried out from a crack in the wall and sat nibbling the cracker. He seemingly had no fear of the human sitting two feet away, watching his every move.

Sam and the mouse had repeated this scene so often over the past few months that she could almost predict the exact moment he would stop eating in order to wash his paws. "Three, two, one," she counted, and then had to wait an extra second before he stopped and began fastidiously licking his paws.

The feed mill was full of rodents trying to get a free meal. It was also full of cats looking to kill said rodents. The fact that this little mouse had survived for so long was a sign of his indomitable spirit. Sam had no temptation to get rid of her visitor, both because he was currently the only friend she had, and because he reminded her of herself. They were both apparently unable to be knocked down, no matter how hard life kept trying.

Sam grimaced and massaged her hip before shifting positions. The doctor who had treated her two years ago assured her she would have no lingering effects after the accident. Apparently he spoke from a textbook and not from experience because her hip often pained her. Occasionally she woke in the night, sweating and whimpering from the excruciating throbbing sensation. Other times, like when it rained, she limped.

But despite the bothersome physical reminder of that horrible day, it was nothing compared to the emotional devastation that lingered inside her.

"What am I doing here?" she asked, not for the first time. She flopped onto her back on the mattress, scaring the mouse into retreat. She blew out a breath, staring at the leaky ceiling. If she had any sense, she would pack her meager belongings and move on. She could go to a bigger city, get a better paying job, maybe even go to college.

Instead, she lingered in this tiny village, working for minimum wage, living in a shack, and dying a little more each day. How much longer could she hold on to the elusive hope that Josh would miraculously forgive her?

A tear dripped into her ear. Not until the leaky wetness made her itch did she realize she was crying. She scrubbed her hand over her face, not attempting to stop her tears, only to wipe them away. She didn't care if she cried in the privacy of her hovel, as long as she maintained her careful reserve in public.

Two years ago, when she had begun working for the Kings, she had worried that her ruse would be unsafe. All her life, she had been surrounded by men who had more machismo than brains, and some of the cowhands on the King spread were no different. If they ever learned she was a girl, her safety could be compromised. But while she had worried over her physical wellbeing, she hadn't given a thought to her emotional health. What could go wrong?

Well, for one, she could fall in love with her boss, which she did the moment he spoke up and defended her. For as long as she lived, she would never forget that moment when Joshua King had looked her up and down, studying her appraisingly. At first, she had almost panicked, thinking he must have guessed her secret.

But then he had stepped away from the wall and cleared his throat. *I want to hire this one, Cam. I think he'll be a good worker.*

Just like that she had been hired by the largest ranch in the area to do what she loved, and the only thing she knew how to do; she would be working with the animals.

As if that hadn't been amazing enough, she had also worked closely with Josh; the only man who had ever stood up for her, the only man who had ever been kind to her, the only man who had ever offered her friendship, the only man she had ever loved.

She supposed some cynics might say the explosive feeling she had felt for Josh on that first day was simply attraction or appreciation. But there was no doubting the way her feelings grew and cemented over the next few months. She had worked with Josh all day, every day, six days a week. They went on roundups together, sleeping out under the stars and talking about their lives. They worked through every kind of weather, looking out for each other in the harsh elements. They worked holidays, weekends, and every other possible scenario imaginable.

She had observed him in every kind of situation, with every kind of person, and he was always the same: serious, thoughtful, and brimming with integrity. He was never two-faced or backhanded, he never lied, he worked harder than anyone else, and he was unfailingly upright in his behavior. Sam had never met anyone like him because she was sure no one else was. After being surrounded with liars and lowlifes for most of her upbringing, Josh's honest nature was like a gift from heaven.

And through everything that occurred, Sam and Josh talked. She opened up to Josh as she never had anyone else, telling him everything, everything except the one thing that mattered most—that she was a woman.

In the beginning, she didn't tell him because she needed the job. She knew as soon as she revealed herself, she would be let go. She had started her job with three dimes in her pocket, and she couldn't afford to be fired.

But by the end of her employment, she didn't reveal herself for a different reason: she knew Josh. She knew how he would react if he found out. The same fastidious nature that served him so well also made him unable to bear dishonesty in anyone else. She knew he would feel betrayed, as if she had purposely lied to him or made a fool of him. That was why, when she had been hit by a car and barely conscious, she had desperately pled not to go to the hospital. If she went to the hospital, Josh would find out, and he would never forgive her. Sadly, that was exactly what happened.

Her thinking was always circular on this subject. If she could go back in time and do it over, would she still pretend to be someone she wasn't in order to get the job? Her conscience wanted to say no; she had hurt the family and lying was wrong, even though it had felt like a necessity at the time for multiple reasons. But if she had never done what she did, she wouldn't have met Josh. And wasn't that worth anything? But by meeting him the way she did, she had caused him to hate her forever.

It was a bittersweet irony that she had finally made a friend, someone she could confide in completely, and now he was lost to her forever because she had withheld one vital piece of information about herself.

Somehow she felt things were drawing to a close. She had waited long enough, hoping for the opportunity to speak with Josh, to apologize and explain. Remaining here for so long was already dangerous.

She needed to move on soon. A little while longer and she would give up, chalk this time in her life up to her greatest failure, and attempt to rebuild. Again.

With that thought in mind, she lost what little appetite she had, which wasn't much to begin with. She had never been one much for food.

You need to put some meat on those bones so you'll look like a real cowboy, Josh had said on more than one occasion, always urging her to eat more. He had been a kind and caring friend to her, and she had repaid him with lies. If she didn't get the chance to make amends, she would regret it for the rest of her life.

She curled on her side and stared at the remainder of the saltine on the floor, wishing her friend would return to keep her company.

* * *

"Do you want to talk about it?" Layla asked as soon as she and Josh were out of town.

"There's nothing to talk about," he said.

"Okay," Layla drawled. "Did you have a nice visit with Chelsea?"

"I always have a nice time with Chelsea. She's a nice girl." He didn't take his eyes off the road as he spoke.

"Josh," Layla started, but didn't know how to continue. She wanted to tell him Sam was a nice girl, too. That she had been caught up in a desperate situation. That he shouldn't take her actions as personally as he had. And most of all that he needed to forgive Sam and release her from the terrible burden of guilt.

As the minutes ticked on the long, silent drive home, Layla had plenty of time to think about the situation with Josh. Forgiveness would go a long way in softening him, she was sure of it. But how to arrange it? Every time Sam had tried to apologize to Josh in the past, he had cut her off by running away. As remote as the ranch was, there hadn't been many opportunities for an encounter.

Layla thought back to when she and Cade were dating. They had a tiff that ended in them not speaking to each other for days. It was Coy who had brought them back together by forcing time together. What Josh and Sam needed was time together, and lots of it.

The more she thought about her plan, the more convinced she was that it was the right course. Josh would never learn to unbend until he learned to forgive. Perhaps the person he needed to forgive the most was Sam. Likewise, Sam seemed to be waiting for Josh to forgive her before she could move on with her life. Maybe this had been the key to Josh's heart all along and none of them had realized it.

By the time they arrived back at the ranch, Layla had a plan. The first step would be to convince the rest of the family to hop on board, and to do that she had to convince Cam. As the head of the family, everyone looked to him for leadership. And the best way to convince Cam was to convince Belle.

Layla smiled because she had arrived at an idea that would not only convince Belle, but it would also solve the problem of how to force togetherness between Josh and Sam. "Brilliant if I do say so myself," she whispered as she walked happily to her house.

CHAPTER 5

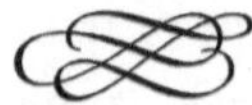

*J*osh exchanged his cowboy boots for running shoes. There was plenty of activity on the ranch to keep him physically fit, but he discovered during his high school baseball days that he enjoyed running for the sake of running.

However, running on a ranch was easier said than done. Between the gopher holes, barbed wire, and cow patties, it was an obstacle course. Instead of utilizing their thousands of acres, he ran down their long dirt lane. It wasn't as rewarding as pounding the flat pavement of his high school track course, but the end result was the same—less stress.

Except this time it didn't seem to be working. This was the third time he had run since the meeting in the drugstore, and he was still wound as tightly as he had been then.

Why wouldn't he go away? *She,* he mentally corrected himself with a grimace. In his mind, Sam was still the guy who had been his best friend. Her hair was long now, brushing her shoulders, but that did nothing to erase the image in his head. He still pictured the little guy with the big eyes and too-big cowboy hat whenever he thought of Sam. And the image still hurt a second before the searing anger returned to overshadow any other emotion. How could he have lied that way? *She.*

If ever Josh's anger at Sam started to recede, he would remember all the time spent together and all the intimate talks they had shared. He had slept not more than a foot away from her on multiple occasions. He had shared a hotel room with her. He had used the bathroom in front of her, for crying out loud. Though in retrospect, Sam had studiously looked away. At the time, Josh had found his privacy issues amusing. Now he found them enraging, like everything else.

How she must have laughed at him all those embarrassing times when Josh showed none of the modesty he normally reserved for the female of the species. Having grown up with three brothers and a slew of ranch hands, he was used to being himself around men, not bothering to observe the necessary code of conduct for mixed company. Routinely he had worked without his shirt on, and during the summer he had slept in his boxers whenever they were out overnight.

That thought alone was enough to send him over the edge. He would never, ever think of doing any of those things in front of a girl. At least not a girl who wasn't his wife. And yet Sam had seen it all, and she was nothing to him. Nothing but a liar.

Unbidden, the image of her in the store crept into his mind, causing him to suck air painfully through his already constricted lungs.

Hi, Josh.

She had sounded so hurt, so uncertain, but obviously that had been an act, too. What did she have to be hurt about? She was the perpetrator in this little scheme; he, Josh, was the innocent victim.

"Why won't he go away?" he yelled, glad he was in the middle of nowhere and there was no one to observe his breathless ranting. *She,* a voice in his head corrected him. With a growl of frustration, he picked up his speed.

He returned to the house, breathless, sweaty, and ready for a shower. Not for the first time he wished Belle and Cam were in New York. They shared the main ranch house with him while Coy and Ivy lived in the old, remodeled homestead and Cade and Layla lived in a new house built to accommodate Cade's wheelchair. Josh had at first thought he would be lonely during Belle and Cam's absences, but instead he found he enjoyed the silence and privacy. He could sit on the couch in his boxer shorts and eat frozen burritos for supper whenever he wanted. When Belle was there, he felt the need to observe proper decorum and eat whatever the family happened to be eating that night. Not that Belle wasn't a good cook, because— surprisingly to everyone—she was. And when she was at the ranch she enjoyed indulging her domestic side. Apparently her tiny Manhattan apartment was the size of a dime and didn't lend itself to cooking large meals.

But tonight he wanted to be alone. He wanted to stew in his misery and anger, venting whenever and however he felt like it.

Voices from the kitchen alerted him to the fact that they had a visitor. He hadn't noticed any strange cars out front, so he had no idea who it could be. Certainly no one would walk the forty miles from town to their ranch, so that meant the person had to have hitched a ride with someone. Maybe it was Belle's mom come to stay a couple of days and help Belle get caught up on her work. As a busy and sought-after literary agent, there never seemed to be enough hours in the day for her to get everything done. Whenever she and Cam were in Montana, her mother was a frequent visitor who helped answer phones, type, file, and do whatever else businesswomen needed done. Josh really had no idea; he had only ever worked at the ranch, and he left the business side of things up to Cam and Cade.

Since he was in no condition to greet visitors, grimy as he was, he bypassed the kitchen. But as he was almost to his room, a snatch of conversation caught his ear and caused him to freeze in the hallway. Backing up without turning around, he retraced his steps until he was standing in the doorway of the kitchen, and then he simply stared. He hadn't been imagining things; it had really been Sam's voice he heard.

She, along with his three sisters-in-law, sat at the kitchen table, drinking tea, talking and laughing like old friends.

Despite the fact that he was hot and sweaty, something within Josh went cold at the sight. They were up to something. Facing down one of his brothers' wives was always a formidable task, but when the three of them banded together, they were unstoppable.

As a unit, they turned to look at him. Sam remained staring down at her cup, her shoulders stiff and her hands tense.

"Josh," Ivy said, her sweet southern accent working to soften him slightly for whatever was about to happen.

"What's going on?" he asked. His mouth was dry and he chewed his tongue, trying to generate enough saliva to speak properly.

"We've been talking," Layla said.

"We need more help out here," Ivy added.

"We need a secretary," Belle said.

He relaxed slightly. If they wanted to hire Sam as a secretary, it was bad, but not horrible. He spent most of his time on the range. The office was a place he rarely set foot. He sensed they were awaiting his reaction. "You're going to share a secretary?"

"Well," Layla began, "I don't need one right now, but I will when I figure out what I want to do next."

"I only need one a couple hours a week to enter some information into my breeding software," Ivy said.

"Mostly, she'll be mine. My mother is getting really tired of being my occasional secretary."

He had no idea why they were explaining all this to him; he didn't care. "Okay." He said. He tried to ease out of the doorway, but they were still pinning him with a collective stare.

"There's more," Belle said. Now it was her turn to stare intently at her mug. "I really need someone here to be at my beck and call to coordinate this office with my New York office."

"Mmm, hmm," he said, wishing she would get to the point so he could grab a shower.

"I mean that literally. I need someone to be *here*." She tapped the table and looked up at him. "And, no offense, but the house could really use some help when we're gone. Not that you're a slob, Josh. But this place needs a woman's touch on a fulltime basis."

It was difficult to hear her over the sudden buzzing sensation in his ears. He looked at the three women who were facing him, their expressions a combination of love and defiance. Then he glanced at Sam who still remained hunched over her mug of tea. And he did the only reasonable thing he could do; he turned and ran from the house.

CHAPTER 6

"Stop laughing," Josh said for the second time.

His brothers were in the office, and they had been laughing for a good two minutes.

"It's so funny," Coy said. He was doubled over with his arm crossed over his stomach. He wiped his eyes and sniffed.

"What's funny about telling you to control your wives?" Josh asked, but the question had the undesired effect of sending them into more peals of laughter. As he was about to give up and stalk from the office, Cade managed to pull himself together enough to be serious.

"Did you ever consider maybe it's not all about you, Josh?"

"Right," Josh said. "I can tell when they're plotting. They've got that look."

"Maybe what they're plotting has as much to do with Sam as it does with you," Cam said.

"What are you talking about?" Josh asked angrily, sure they were trying to pull something over on him.

"Look, my wife is an orphan," Cade began. "She has a heart for other girls who are alone like she was. There's no one more alone than Sam. Layla cried when she found out Sam was living in that slum behind the mill. She *cried*, Josh. You try saying no to that."

"And you know Belle can't stand to see a brilliant mind go to waste," Cam added. "We all know Sam is meant for greater things than being the checkout girl at the pharmacy. The girls want to take her on as their new project. They have big things in mind for our little Sam."

"She's not 'our little Sam,'" Josh snapped. "Have you forgotten how she lied to us? How she tricked us all those months?"

"No," Cam said evenly. "But what harm did it do, really? Wasn't she still a good worker? I paid her to work, and she did that work with excellence. I'm sorry about the way things ended, but I couldn't have asked for a better employee."

"What harm did it do?" Josh echoed. "She lied to us. She *lied*."

"Did she really?" Coy asked. "I went back and checked her employment records. They never once stated she was a male. On her tax statement she left that portion blank."

"She knew what we assumed, and she let us," Josh said. He was furious with his family for taking her side.

"That's true," Cade said. "But maybe she had a good reason."

"There's never a good reason for lying," Josh said.

"Josh, if you continue to look at the world as black and white, you're bound to either be disillusioned or frustrated. Yes, lying is wrong. But sometimes people make bad decisions out of fear or desperation. If we're not willing to extend them a little grace, then we can't expect much grace for ourselves when we mess up," Cade said.

"There's a simple solution to that equation, Cade," Josh said. "Don't mess up in the first place."

"Ugh," Coy said. "Talking to you is like beating our heads against brick. Since you're unwilling to listen to reason, let me break it down into the simplest terms. Sam is hired, and she's going to be living here for as long as our wives say. The end. If you're not mature enough to deal with seeing her on a daily basis, you can make other arrangements."

A tense silence fell over the room as everyone waited for Josh's reaction. "If you're not men enough to rein in your wives, maybe I will find somewhere else."

"If you think the definition of a man is ordering others around and getting your own way all the time, you are sadly mistaken," Cade said.

Though Coy was the one who initially threw down the gauntlet, he couldn't take the tension anymore. "If someone says 'if' one more time, I'm going to lose it." Cam and Cade chuckled, Josh didn't. "Look, Josh, the point is that we're all in agreement on this. It isn't only the women. Cade, Cam and I feel like Samantha needs a break, and we're the best ones to provide one for her. We have the means and the opportunity, and we sort of owe her."

Josh was taken aback by hearing Sam's full name. For that reason, his answer was softer than it otherwise would have been. "How do you figure we owe her?" he asked quietly.

"Because she was hit by a car while working for us, and we dumped her off to fend for herself."

Josh stood straighter, his fists clenched at his sides. "We paid for her care. Cam sent a transport to bring her back to town. He even paid her during her recovery. What more could we have done?"

"We could have taken care of her ourselves," Cam said. "At the time, we all respected your feelings on the matter, but I regret that we didn't get personally involved in her care. Now that I know what her living conditions were during her convalescence..." He paused and shook his head. "Well, it's not right."

"What do you mean her living conditions? Because she lived alone doesn't mean she needed care. Lots of people manage fine on their own. The doctor said there was nothing broken and no permanent damage."

Coy rubbed a weary hand over his face. "Josh, she could barely move for six weeks, and she was living in that tiny hovel with a bare mattress on the floor. Where is your compassion?"

Josh's conscience pinged, but he didn't let it show. "It appears to me she made it fine."

Coy opened his mouth to speak again, but Cam preempted him. "Nevertheless, the decision has been made. Samantha stays. If you don't like it, you can go."

Josh looked at them, sitting in a semi-circle across from where he stood. "You would choose a stranger over your own brother."

"We would choose doing what's right rather than supporting your immature grudge," Cade said.

"So be it," Josh said. He turned, stalked back to the house, and took a shower. When his shower was finished, he hopped in his truck and drove to town.

* * *

Sam, still sitting in the kitchen with Layla, Ivy, and Belle, winced when she heard him slam out of the house.

"Are you sure about this?" she asked the group at large. "I don't want to cause problems in your family."

"We're positive about this," Layla said. "We need someone, and you're the one we want.

"I've never been a secretary before," Sam said uncertainly.

"I had no idea how to keep house before I came here," Layla volunteered. "You'll learn, and you'll do great."

"And I'm going to teach you everything you need to know in order to be my secretary," Belle said.

"First things first, you'll need a new wardrobe," Ivy said.

Sam bit her lip. "I only have a small amount in savings. I'm not sure how many clothes that would cover."

"The wardrobe is part of your salary," Belle explained. "There may be times some of my clients pay a visit to the ranch. Or an occasion might arise where I'll take you to New York with me. You'll need to look professional."

"Plus, clothes are my thing," Ivy said, all enthusiasm now. "Fashion and makeup are my hobby. Let me indulge my passion."

"It's true," Layla added. "She gave me a makeover as soon as she and Coy were married."

Sam nodded and tried not to look as overwhelmed as she felt. Clothes? Makeup? *New York?* She had always dreamed of visiting the big city, but never in her wildest imaginings did she think she would

36

be going as a personal secretary to the sophisticated and successful Belle Landry King. She had the sudden urge to back out of the room and sprint away until she reached somewhere far and safe. Always before, she had thought she remained stuck in her dead-end job because she couldn't afford to do something else. Maybe the real reason was because she was afraid to take a chance.

Why should she be afraid, though? These women had made it, and they weren't so much different than her. Belle was from this tiny town, and yet she had made a name for herself in New York's competitive publishing world. Ivy had moved half a country away from her family, started her horse-breeding business from scratch, and it was thriving. And Layla was an orphan who survived a murder attempt and went on to start a candy company that sold for a tidy profit. If they could succeed, maybe Sam could too. All she needed was someone to teach her what to do, and right now she had three fairy godmothers who were offering to do exactly that.

"I can't ever possibly repay you for what you're doing for me," she said, tears clogging her throat.

"Don't try," Belle said. "Some day you'll have the chance to help some other girl who needs it. Remember this moment and pay it forward."

Sam nodded. Knowing how it felt to be on the receiving end of so much generosity, she was anxious to someday be able to be the one doing the giving. The other three women appeared to take her nod as tacit agreement because almost as soon as she finished, they swept her into the office and began making her over.

"What size are you? What size shoes? How tall are you? Are your eyes that blue, or do you wear contacts? Have you ever worn makeup? When is the last time you had your hair cut?" And on and on the questions went until Sam's head was spinning. They all spoke at once, not waiting for her to answer before they moved on to something else. Belle scanned the computer while Ivy stood over her shoulder giving directions. Layla began making a list on a piece of paper, presumably of what Sam would need.

Sam stood back, watching in awe. She wondered if they would

notice if she simply backed out of the room. Her mother had been nothing like these women. Though she had been a popular performer with the rodeo, she had also been terribly insecure. Seemingly the only way she could feel good about herself had been by having a man at her side. As if that weren't bad enough, the men she chose depreciated as the years went by.

She only had vague memories of the father who had been killed in a car accident when Sam was three, but most of those memories involved him yelling. After that, there had been a progressively worse parade of boyfriends until at last her mother married the man who had been Sam's stepfather and worst nightmare.

There had been other women in her life, friends of her mother and girlfriends of her stepfather, but they had all been very much like Sam's mother—at the mercy of the men in their lives. But these women, though they were married to three strong, mule-headed cowboys, seemed to find security within themselves. Each had her own identity, and each was strong in her own way. To Sam, who had also always been at the mercy of some man (though not by choice), their confidence was baffling. What made them who they were, and how could she be like them?

Of course her primary goal here was to try and gain forgiveness from Josh. But maybe, just maybe, she could gain something for herself in the process. She could get career experience. She could travel. And, most important, she could learn to be like the three women who sat before her: strong, confident, and independent.

CHAPTER 7

"Josh," Chelsea exclaimed, shocked speechless by his unexpected appearance on her doorstep. "Did we have a date?"

"No. I just…I just wanted to see you."

She had to work hard to hide her reaction to that statement. She and some friends had been planning to go clubbing in the city, and she wasn't anxious to break those plans. "That's so sweet," she said, betraying none of her inner turmoil over his presence. "How long can you stay?"

He shrugged. "I don't really have any plans."

She bit back an impatient frown. "Great. We can hang out all night." Did he really think she did nothing on the nights they weren't together? Did he think she sat around and longed for him while he was in the boonies working with his cattle or his stupid dogs? She hoped so because that was the illusion she tried to create.

She opened the screen, grasped his hand, and tugged him inside. He followed her like the stupid fish he was. They walked down the hall to the least shabby room in the house. So far Josh hadn't seemed to notice the poverty of his surroundings, mostly because she carefully staged the setting with dim lights and candles whenever he was due to arrive. Now he looked too preoccupied to notice much besides his own sullen mood.

"Sit down and I'll get you some iced tea," she said sweetly. He sat and she walked to the kitchen, shooting a glance over her shoulder to make sure he obeyed and stayed put like a good boy. After assuring herself he was still in the living room, she reached for the phone from the wall and dialed her best friend.

"Hey," she whispered, cupping her hand over the mouthpiece. "Call me back in a minute."

"Why?" Hillary asked, sounding bored.

"Josh is here and I want to get rid of him."

"What's he doing there?" Hillary asked, sounding as indignant as Chelsea felt. Josh should know his place; he shouldn't show up out of the blue when they didn't have a date. That type of behavior was fine during the middle of the afternoon when she was at work; his visits helped relieve the boredom. But nighttime was her time, and she didn't want to be tied down by her too-serious, choirboy boyfriend.

"I don't know," Chelsea said irritably. "But I'm going to get rid of him."

They disconnected without saying goodbye. Chelsea poured the tea and took it back to Josh who looked up at her, unsmiling. "Thank you," he said.

Chelsea wanted to grind her teeth together in annoyance at his morose tone. It wasn't enough that he was the most serious, principled person on the planet. Now he had to be sad, too.

"What's wrong?" she asked, her tone oozing sympathy.

He opened his mouth to speak, shook his head, and took a sip of tea. Chelsea studied him, thinking she liked him better when he said nothing at all. No doubt he was beautiful. That had been the first thing that attracted her to him, followed closely by his family's net worth. The King brothers were all nice looking, but Josh outshone them all. His hair was more blond than brown and his eyes were almost green with flecks of gold and brown. On the occasions when he did smile, he had two deep dimples that gave him a boyish, angelic look. But his body didn't conjure the angel image; years of ranch work had left him ripped. He was tall, too. She had always liked tall guys.

Finally, he appeared to be about to confess whatever stupid thing was upsetting him, but her phone rang.

"Excuse me," she said regretfully. She left the room, picked up the phone, and held a fake conversation while Hillary said outrageous things on the other end of the line. After a minute, she hung up the phone and returned to the living room.

"That was my grandma. She's sick and wants me to come spend the evening with her, taking care of her."

Josh's face softened into a mask of concern. "Is there anything I can do? Maybe I could go with you."

It took effort for Chelsea not to roll her eyes. If this town possessed a Boy Scout troop, Josh would have made it all the way to Eagle Scout. "That's really sweet, Josh, but you know how touchy my grandma is about the subject of my boyfriends. I'm afraid it would invite a lot of lectures, and I don't want to stress her out that way." In reality, her family loved Josh and practically fell all over themselves every time they saw him, but he fell for her excuse like the dope he was.

"I understand," he said gravely, nodding. "At least let me drive you over there."

She opened her mouth to protest, then thought better of it. Josh wasn't as stupid as she liked to pretend he was. It never hurt to keep up the pretense as much as possible. "That would be great," she said, smiling sweetly. She would pop in to say hello to her grandmother and have her friends pick her up there.

He waited on the porch, making sure she locked the door, then held the truck door for her and lifted her up. He was quiet on the short drive to her grandmother's house. She thought he was probably upset over whatever was bugging him, but to be on the safe side, she turned and gave him a kiss when the truck pulled to a stop.

He reached for her, drawing her close and intensifying the kiss to a surprising degree. If there was one thing she liked about Josh, it was that he didn't kiss like a choirboy. Eventually she was the one who pulled away, fearing that her grandmother might actually be watching them disapprovingly from the house, alerted by the unexpected arrival of a truck. What if she came out to say hello? That would definitely be awkward.

"I should go," she said reluctantly. "See you later, baby."

Josh, looking much happier than when he arrived, gave her one final peck on the cheek and waved her away. He sighed as he put his truck into gear and drove away. Thank goodness for the honest wholesomeness of Chelsea; she was a soothing balm after the unsettling sight of that liar Sam McCoy.

* * *

SAM WAS TIRED. Who knew overhauling her life would be so exhausting? On her very first day, Cam and Coy had driven her to town to retrieve her things. It hadn't taken long to pack up her meager belongings. In fact, everything fit in one black garbage bag. Her tiny apartment was as clean as she could make it, but she was still embarrassed over its decrepit state, as well as her lack of belongings. Stuffing one's possessions into a trash sack wasn't exactly a classy thing to do.

The King brothers didn't say a word, but she wondered what they were thinking because both of them had their lips pressed tightly together in a grim line, even Coy who was usually always smiling.

Although they would probably never understand, leaving the little slum was difficult for Sam in some ways. It represented all the safety and security she had in the world. Even though she was going to a much better place, she was also heading toward the unknown. This apartment, ugly and dumpy though it was, was within her comfort zone. Having grown up in trailers her whole life, she was used to small spaces. Being at the King's vast spread would be like setting free a bird that has been in captivity its whole life: overwhelming.

The brothers turned toward the door, but Sam paused, sweeping the small space with one glance. Then she walked back to the cupboard, took out her plastic container of crackers, opened it, and laid it on its side in front of the mouse's opening in the wall.

"Goodbye," she whispered.

As if he heard and understood what was going on, the mouse poked its head out of the wall and blinked up at her with giant eyes and twitching whiskers. Realistically, he was drawn by the food, but Sam liked to think he was saying goodbye to her and would miss her as much as she would miss him, though the thought caused her eyes to mist embarrassingly. She backed out of the room to give herself the chance to blink her tears away before she turned to face the Kings.

Coy helped her into the truck while Cam drove and no one said a word on the long trip to the ranch. Sam was thankful for the peaceful silence. She was sad and anxious, and she didn't feel like making idle small talk. She had no idea why the brothers remained silent. Coy especially was a chatty person. Maybe they knew and understood that she needed the quiet. If so, it was very thoughtful of them to provide it.

When she arrived back at the house, Layla helped her unpack her things.

"This is my old room," Layla said. "It has its own bathroom. Josh is across the hall, then there are two empty rooms, and Cam and Belle have the suite at the end of the hall."

Sam stood back, watching Layla efficiently arrange her things in the chest of drawers. She felt that she should help, but there wasn't room for two people, and Layla seemed intent on doing the task herself for some reason. At last Sam noticed Layla's hands were shaking, but she didn't realize she was crying until she stopped and bent over a drawer.

"I'm sorry," she said. "It's so like the first time I arrived here; it's dredging up a lot of memories for me. I had nothing and no one. Then I came here and found a home and a family." She turned to look at Sam. "I hope the same thing will happen for you."

Sam smiled and nodded, but didn't reply. The difference between their situations was that Layla had found Cade, and Cade loved her very much. There was only one brother left unattached, and his loathing of her was palpable. She had no delusions about her station here. She was an employee who would eventually move on when the situation became unbearable. But for now she was here, and she might as well learn to relax and enjoy it.

There was no time to relax, however. Belle was very kind, and very funny, but she was also very efficient. As soon as Sam exited her room, her training began.

"We ordered a new wardrobe for you. It should be delivered in a few days. I know it's odd to have other people pick out your clothes, but if Ivy wasn't a horse breeder, she would probably be a personal shopper. I think you'll be surprised by how much you like the clothes."

She didn't allow Sam the opportunity to say that anything besides her normal discount store clothing would be a step up.

"First off, let me show you how the phone works. Are you familiar with computers? Can you type?" And so it had begun. For the last week, things hadn't slowed down at all until today. Most likely Belle would have kept working, but Cam reminded her it was Saturday and Sam had been working six days straight with no breaks. Almost reluctantly, Belle had told Sam to take the rest of the day off and relax.

Now Sam found herself at loose ends, trying to remember and process all that had happened during the week. She wasn't yet perfect at her new job, but she wanted to be. She downloaded a typing program from the internet and planned to practice it as soon as Belle left for New York. Belle had once let it slip that her New York secretary typed ninety words per minute. If that was the case, Sam intended to type a hundred. She had no idea she was competitive or a perfectionist, but apparently she was because she wanted to be the best, most perfect secretary Belle had ever had.

That was why, even though she meandered around the ranch, she wasn't paying attention to where she was going or what she was doing. Instead, she was mentally planning what she needed to do during Belle's absence in order to stay on top of the work that could so quickly pile up. Sam was astounded that any one woman could be so important or have so much work to do. And she wasn't the only one who was astounded; Cam had complained more than once that his wife's workload was too heavy.

"I could drop an author," Belle had said with a significant tone Sam didn't understand. Apparently Cam did, because he shut up and didn't complain again.

"Well, look who it is."

Sam stopped short when the voice spoke. Somehow she had stumbled upon the bunkhouse and was now face to face with someone she used to work with every day.

"Hello, Tanner," she said, nervously smoothing down one of her new pairs of pants.

"If it isn't Sam the man," Tanner continued. Behind him, the rest of the cowboys exited the bunker and surrounded her in a semi-circle. Most of them had been here two years ago, but a few were new.

"I…I suppose I owe you an apology," she said. She was unaccountably nervous at the sight of so many men staring her down. How angry were they? What if they decided to attack her and "teach her a lesson?" She would have no defense against so many of them, and she was too far from the house for anyone to hear her screams. She backed up a step, swallowing nervously.

Tanner, seeing that she was petrified, smiled. "I'm teasing you, Sam. Who cares if you pretended to be a man? We're the stupid ones for believing you. Do you have any idea how hard I laughed at myself for passing off so many odd things as your quirky nature?"

She smiled and clasped her hands behind her back. "I'm sorry, just the same. I never meant to deceive or hurt anyone. At the time, it seemed like the only way."

"You were a scared eighteen-year-old kid. Forget about it. How are you doing since the accident? How are things in the main house?" He leaned against the doorframe. The other cowboys meandered away once they were sure no drama was about to unfold.

"I'm fine. The house is nice. The Kings are very good employers."

Tanner nodded. "That they are." He looked behind him and took a step outside, towards Sam. "Look, Sam," he said more softly, leaning down so she could hear him. "You shouldn't come over here anymore. Some of the new guys…well, let's say I don't trust them near a pretty young girl. I do what I can to keep an eye on them, but I'm not here all the time, you know?"

She cast a frightened glance toward the bunkhouse. "I won't come back. I didn't mean to come here today, but I wasn't paying attention to where I was going. Thanks for the warning, Tanner."

He grinned at her. "You're a good kid. Keep out of trouble."

She nodded and backed away another step before turning to sprint to the house. Then she remembered she was wearing a pair of her new fancy shoes, so instead of running she walked as quickly as she could. So intent was she on reaching the house again, that she almost ran into a horse, not even noticing its rider until he spoke.

"Stay away from the bunkhouse," Josh said coldly. "If there's one thing Cam won't tolerate, it's you flirting with the ranch hands and getting them all riled up." After he made his proclamation and rode away, Sam realized he hadn't looked at her once, keeping his eyes straight ahead as if she weren't worth the effort to look down.

Previously, she would have been devastated by his treatment, but in addition to learning her job this week, she had tried to learn how to be like the three King women. So instead of allowing Josh's hurtful words to wound her, she allowed them to make her angry.

"If you want me to stay away from the bunkhouse, why don't you get down off your high horse and make me?" she said. Of course, he was too far gone to hear her mutinous words, but she felt better for having said them. From now on, she was nobody's doormat, not even the high and mighty Joshua King.

CHAPTER 8

On Sunday Cam and Belle returned to New York. Sam had wondered if Belle would feel uncertain about leaving her alone to do her new job, but, after a few last-minute instructions, she said goodbye with a wave and they were gone.

Because it was Sunday, and because her employer would be traveling all day, Sam spent the day relaxing. In the morning, Layla taught her how to make French toast. It was much easier than she thought it would be. After breakfast, the remaining family went to church, but Sam begged off, not wanting to subject Josh to so much time with her. He had been noticeably absent for breakfast as well as for Cam and Belle's goodbye, but Josh never missed church.

The house and ranch were eerily silent with no one working and the family absent. Sam practiced the typing program she had downloaded. She was up to fifty words per minute, but she was still making more mistakes than she liked. After that she spent some time trying on all the new clothes that had arrived for her throughout the week. As Belle had predicted, Ivy did an excellent job picking the clothes. They were exactly what Sam would have picked for herself if she knew where to find them and had money enough to pay for them.

In addition to several classy-looking pant suits and tailored blouses, there were a couple pairs of jeans, khakis, sweaters, socks, shoes, and even some dresses.

These Sam set on the bed reverently, almost too awed to touch them. She hadn't owned many dresses in her life, and certainly none for the last four years. For two years of her life she had pretended to be a boy, and there had always been a part of her that yearned for the pretty, feminine things other girls wore. She hated wearing the boxy men's clothing. But at the time, she hadn't been aiming for prettiness; she had been aiming for safety.

Since it was Sunday, and since she so badly wanted to try one on, she slipped off her jeans and put on one of the pretty dresses. The dress nipped in at her waist before flaring to her knees. Sam felt like a little girl as she spun in front of the mirror, making the dress flare. It was so *pretty.* Immediately she decided that when she earned enough money to buy things for herself, she would buy more dresses. And maybe some skirts. And possibly a pair of high heels. Not that the pantsuits Ivy had ordered weren't feminine, because they were. But nothing had ever made her feel as girly or as pretty as the dress she was wearing now. She wished she had somewhere to go or something to do, but she didn't. The ranch was an hour from anywhere by car, and she didn't have a car. The Kings had told her to help herself to one of the ranch trucks whenever she wanted, but she didn't yet feel comfortable doing that. Not only because she still felt like a guest, but also because she hadn't driven in a long time and her skills were too rusty to attempt the twisty back roads leading to town.

Belatedly she realized she could have gone for a horse ride this afternoon. After having worked at the ranch in the capacity of a cowboy, she felt comfortable saddling a horse and riding by herself, but now that she was wearing the pretty dress she didn't want to take it off and put her jeans back on. She could still visit the horses, though. Horses had always had a calming, cheering effect on her, from the time she was a little girl and used to delight in petting her mother's horse.

Her mother was on her mind as she walked to the corral. Maybe that was why instead of going to the barn with the working horses, she meandered toward the special corral that contained Ivy's stallion.

Ivy's father had gifted her with two purebred horses whose parentage could be traced back to horses owned by European royalty hundreds of years ago. Josh had once told her that stallion alone was worth more than half the family's cows put together. That was why it had its own barn and corral. It was also why the stallion's barn was the only one secured with a lock at night. Though no one had spoken the thought out loud, Sam had the impression all the brothers were a little nervous to have such an expensive horse on the property. It might prove too tempting for a rustler who knew the animal's worth.

The stallion was out in its corral, proudly prancing in a circle. He stopped at the opposite side of the enclosure and eyed Sam suspiciously. Sam expected nothing less; the horse wasn't known for his friendliness. He was incredibly beautiful, fast, and strong, however, which was why he was such a hot commodity. Friendliness could be bred through the mares. What this horse possessed could be found few other places. He could run for miles without growing weary and carry a rider without breaking a sweat. Besides that, he was healthy. His genetic testing had showed few flaws that might be passed on to future generations. In his younger days, he had won the prestigious Belmont race before he had been retired as a sire.

Sam made no move to call to him; she was content to simply glory in the beauty of such a majestic creature. But to her surprise the horse walked over to her. Standing a foot away, he looked down at her and snorted. She had the sudden, irrational desire to curtsy to him for bestowing such an honor on her. Instead, she tentatively reached her hand up to scratch behind his ear. He shied away from her and shook his head. Her hand froze for a second before continuing.

At last she reached him and began scratching. The horse closed its eyes and nickered in delight. Sam wanted to laugh, but she was afraid of startling him.

"You old softie," she muttered instead. "You're only pretending to be mean and standoffish. What you need is lots of love and affection, huh?"

The horse whinnied again as if affirming her statement. That was also the exact moment that Josh appeared unexpectedly to her left.

* * *

For the first time in his life, Josh skipped church. When he was sixteen and his parents moved to Arizona, one of the promises he had made in order to be left behind was that he would faithfully attend church every week. All the brothers had made the same promise to their mother, and all of them had kept it unless something dire came along. Nothing had ever been dire enough to keep Josh from going. Until today.

He thought Sam might go, and he couldn't stand the thought of two hours in the car with her, along with all that time spent in church together. No doubt people were already talking about the unusual situation with their new employee. No need to add fuel to the gossip fire by attending with her and sitting beside her.

Instead he decided to have his own version of church on the range. He had often thought that the beauty of Montana was proof enough of God's existence. How could anyone look at the grandeur of the landscape and think he was alone in the world? More than once, Josh had shared a poignant moment with nature that convinced him not only that God was real, but that God cared about him.

But when he returned after a two-hour ride and saw Sam standing in front of Ivy's corral, he began to wish he had chosen to attend church instead. Had she stayed home to irritate him and ruin his day? He had become adept at avoiding her during the week. He rose earlier than anyone else in the house and then kept to himself, working hard until he was too exhausted to think. Then he showered and drove into town.

Chelsea was sadly unavailable most nights, due to her family commitments. He was disappointed by her loss, but he was happy she was such a devoted family girl. With her gone, he spent some time with his old high school friends, took in a couple of movies and, a few times, ended up at the library reading ranching magazines.

Maybe it was because he had been so good at avoiding Sam that the sight of her came as a shock now. She stood on her toes at the fence, scratching that infernally mean stallion of Ivy's. Josh knew for a fact that no one but Ivy was allowed close enough to touch the devil, but there was Sam, looking for all the world like she had made a new best friend. For some reason the sight irritated him. Why should animals like her so much? Weren't they supposed to be good judges of character? Then again, the horse was evil. Maybe like was attracted to like.

But as he rode up to her, prepared to chastise her for anything he could think of, the wind was sucked from his lungs, along with the moisture in his suddenly dry mouth. Sam was wearing a dress. Sam was *beautiful*.

The information was even more shocking because he had never noticed before. How could he not have noticed that she was lovely? The dress was blue, echoing the deep blue of her eyes. Her dark hair skimmed her shoulders. Her cheeks were a rosy pink, but maybe that was simply because she was looking up at him, waiting for him to speak.

But, as hard as he tried, Josh couldn't conjure a word. All he could think was that, once again, Sam had somehow flown under his radar and kept something vitally important from him. Of course he knew it was irrational to blame her for keeping her prettiness a secret. Except for the dress she didn't look much different than she did every other day.

He frowned. Maybe that was the problem; maybe he didn't look at her every other day. Whenever they met, he did his best not to look at her. Consequently, the vision he carried of her in his head was the one of her as she had been when she worked on the ranch—a tiny cowboy with roughly chopped hair and shoddy clothes. But that vision bore no resemblance to the flower of a girl now gazing shyly up at him. For this one moment at least, his anger at her fled. How could he be angry at something so exquisite?

He dismounted his horse and led it behind him, closing the gap between them. "Come with me," he said. Then, not waiting to see if she followed his order, he turned and headed toward the barn.

CHAPTER 9

Sam wanted to disobey, she really did. The newly found independent part of her wanted to turn tail and head back to the house with her head in the air. But the curious part of her won out. What could Josh possibly want?

No doubt he wanted to yell at her for something or other. She had no idea why he didn't simply get it over with there in the yard, but maybe he wanted privacy. Quickly, she scanned the horizon. Maybe he had seen someone watching them, but she didn't see anyone besides the horse who looked put out that Sam had stopped scratching him.

"Later," she assured him. Then she turned and followed Josh to the barn. If he was going to yell at her, he was going to be mighty surprised when she didn't stand still and take it. She had a few things that needed to be said as well, and she would make him listen.

But when she reached the barn, she didn't see him. She stood on her toes trying to see over the tops of the stalls.

"Down here," Josh called. She followed the sound of his voice to a stall about two thirds of the way down the barn. The door was slightly ajar but not until she opened it and stepped inside did she see why he was sitting down.

"Oh," she said softly, delightedly. One of Josh's Australian cattle dogs had given birth to six puppies, and if their tiny size and unopened eyes were any indication, it hadn't been that long ago.

"When did this happen?" she asked.

"This morning," he said, his tone tender as he looked at his beloved pets. The dogs were his project, and his alone. He had brought them to the ranch as an experiment. He alone took care of them, and he was also responsible for training them to respond to his commands and hone their natural cattle-herding instincts. Seeing him with the dogs allowed a rare glimpse into the hidden soft side most people didn't know he possessed.

"Sit down," he invited. He moved aside to make room for her in the hay. She took a step forward and paused when the mother dog growled at her. The dogs were known for their possessive, protective natures.

"Easy girl," Josh said, giving her head a gentle pat where it lay on the hay. "It's just Sam. You know her."

Either the dog responded to Josh's words, or she caught Sam's familiar scent because she lay back and relaxed. Or at least she relaxed as much as she could with six tiny pups suckling her.

"They're so beautiful," Sam breathed. She had always thought the adult dogs looked a bit mangy and intimidating with their short speckled coats and icy blue eyes. But the puppies were pudgy little balls of fur. "I didn't know you intended to breed them."

"I didn't," Josh said wryly. "Apparently they had their own agenda where breeding was concerned." He sighed. "I didn't expect the litter to be this large. I was hoping if they only had a couple of puppies, Cam would let me keep them all. But six more dogs is a few too many. I'm going to hate to see them go, though." The puppies finished their meal and began stumbling blindly through the hay, looking for a comfortable place to sleep. Josh picked one up and handed it to Sam.

"Oh," she said again, closing her eyes in delight.

Josh studied her as if he had never seen her before, and he wasn't certain he ever had. Was this really the same person he had spent so many months sharing his life with? How, how, *how* had he missed the fact that she was a woman? Every gesture and expression was drenched in femininity. Had she always been like this? If so, how blind and stupid could he be to have missed it?

His old anger began to return to the surface. For the moment, he repressed it. He was having a nice time right now, and so was she. For as long as he could stand it, he would pretend she was a pretty stranger and nothing more. Separating this Sam from the Sam who had betrayed him was easier than it should have been, he thought.

He watched in wonder as the puppy she was holding began to whimper. She settled it over her heart and cupped her hands around it to keep it warm and it instantly settled down and fell asleep. The sight made him remember the story Coy had told him earlier in the week, that when he and Cam went to retrieve Sam's things, they had found her living in something that looked as if it was from a third world country—a tiny shack with barely running water and leaky everything. In fact it had no indoor plumbing beyond the sink in the makeshift kitchen. The owners left a key to the mill and if Sam had to use the restroom in the night, she had to exit her apartment and enter the darkened, locked feed mill. That was also where she had to shower every day, which meant she had to wake up, get dressed, pack her amenities, tramp through the mill, shower, re-dress, and walk back to her apartment to finish getting ready. Coy had also told them that a brazen little mouse shared her living quarters and that Sam had seemed to accept him as a friend, even leaving crackers for him when she moved out.

He had a difficult time reconciling the vision before him with the Sam who had survived for two years in that hovel. Now she looked healthy and happy as she cuddled the puppy and cooed softly to Nikita, the mother dog. Nikita thumped her tail happily as she listened to Sam's soothing words telling her what a good job she had done and what a good mother she was.

Josh looked away, toward the wall. Coy had also said there was no insulation in the shack and a lone electric heater against the wall. That she had survived their harsh winters in that environment was a miracle. He had the sudden desire to pick Sam up and nestle her against his heart the same way she had done for the puppy. Unfortunately, his generous mood was short-lived.

"Josh, are we ever going to talk about it?" Sam asked gently.

And just like that the moment was over. All his old anger, resentment, and suspicion returned to the surface. Maybe Sam had been playing on his sympathies all along. Maybe her apartment hadn't been as bad as Coy described. After all, Coy was a bleeding heart and a sucker for any hard-luck story. Wasn't it possible Sam had taken him in with her big blue eyes and tiny physique? Right now she looked like she needed to be taken care of. But two years ago she looked like a man who could take care of herself. One of those personas was real, and one was a lie. How was he to know which was which? No matter what he wouldn't be taken in by her again.

"No," he answered abruptly. Then he stood and walked out of the barn.

* * *

STUPID, *stupid, stupid, Sam,* she chastised herself. She shouldn't have pushed; it was too soon. But the temptation to clear the air had been too tempting. For the first time in two years, Josh had been the way he was during the course of their friendship: soft, open, and kind. Nowadays Sam barely recognized the hardened stranger he had become. Today was her first glimpse at the man she sometimes thought she had imagined. Had she misconstrued Josh's once protective kindness toward her? Sometimes she thought she must have been so desperate for friendship that she had made everything up. Worse, sometimes she feared she was so like her mother that she had seen Josh as she wanted to see him, and not as he actually was.

But today had proved to her the kind and compassionate friend she loved was still in there somewhere, buried deep under those hardened layers. And the fact that she was the one responsible for creating that tough exterior shell was even more motivation to keep her fighting to reveal the person she knew he could be, the person he had once been with her.

After some probing this week, she had learned what it had been like for Josh after her accident, what her deception had done to him. He had returned home from Wyoming shocked, disheartened, and disillusioned. Quietly, he had relayed the facts of her accident to Cam and when Cam questioned him over leaving her injured and alone in the hospital, Josh had left without answering. After that, no one saw him for two days. He had taken his horse and gone camping on a remote corner of the property, fishing and living off the land.

When he returned, no one spoke of it again until two weeks later. One of their cowboys poked fun at him. Josh had taken a swing at him and probably would have beaten him up if Coy and Tanner hadn't physically restrained him. After that, no one mentioned Sam's name for two years until that day a week ago when Layla made the suggestion they bring her to the ranch for a job.

Sam still didn't understand that part of things, and no one had explained it to her. "But if he hates me so much, why did you bring me here?" she had asked.

"Because it's time to heal," Layla had answered. Sam wasn't sure what that meant; she had no idea how her presence could provide anything but more heartache for Josh, but the family remained adamant about having her here. Because she wanted things to work, and because she was desperate to keep this job, she complied. But she still had her doubts and reservations. And if Josh's reaction today was any indication, she had a right to be wary.

"I'll fix what I've done or die trying," she said to the puppy in her hands. Then she paused and frowned at the little fur ball. Did she mean that flippant statement? Would she be willing to die if it meant providing healing and closure for Josh? She thought of Josh as he had been; laughing and carefree, loving and caring. "Yes," she whispered. "I would die for that." But even as she said the words, she knew it wouldn't come to that. *What could possibly happen to me here? I'm in the safest place in the world.* With that happy thought, she set down her puppy and watched him as he found his mother for another drink of milk.

CHAPTER 10

*J*osh had never been one of those men for whom shutting off his emotions came easily. Sensitive with an overactive conscience, he weighed his decisions carefully, always tried to do the right thing, and agonized over his choices, always wondering if he had chosen wisely. Not for the first time did he envy other men who could seemingly go through life feeling nothing at all. Some people thought he was cold and unfeeling; that was untrue. The reality was that he felt too much. When his emotions boiled over and became too much to handle, he turned to his old friend anger.

Anger was so strong it could overpower any other emotion, say, guilt over a bad decision. Or betrayal because you found out your best friend had been lying to you for the entirety of your relationship. Or confusion—Josh was especially good at using anger to cover confusion.

That last cover-up explained why he was so angry right now; because he was actually very confused. His hard-won anger at Sam was starting to dissolve, leaving in its place a disconcerting attraction he didn't want and couldn't understand. He didn't want Sam; he wanted Chelsea, and he had her. Why, then, did he spend half the night lying awake, staring at the ceiling, and picturing Sam's big blue eyes widening with delight at her first glimpse of the puppies? Why did he keep seeing the way she smiled when the puppy nudged itself under her neck? Why couldn't he seem to conjure one detail about Chelsea, no matter how hard he tried?

That fact only added to his anger. Chelsea was his girlfriend; Josh owed it to her to be faithful, both in thought and deed. Irrational though it was, he couldn't help but blame Sam for his helpless attraction to her. If she wasn't here, he wouldn't be mentally cheating on Chelsea. If only she had stayed far away where it was easy to hate her, everything would be all right.

He scowled at the ceiling. He didn't actually hate her; hate was wrong. What *did* he feel for her? At first he had felt a seething rage at the embarrassment she had caused him. He hated to be laughed at. With Sam's help, he had given everyone a major reason to laugh at him. *Did you really not know she was a girl, Josh?* he had heard on more than one occasion. Usually the question was followed with a guffaw, wink, and nudge. As if Josh and Sam had been carrying on some sort of twisted liaison right under his family's nose. He had tried to remain stoic under the teasing, but when one of his employees made a lewd comment, Josh had had enough. He still felt bad about blowing his top that day.

After some of the initial rage dissipated, the hurt had set in. And the hurt added fuel to the fires of his rage. Whenever he began to feel some mellowing in his attitude toward Sam, he would remember how much she had hurt him, and he would become angry all over again. For two years, anger had been his constant companion and closest friend. It helped to fill the void that Sam left. And it was only fair that he use it against her because it was her fault the anger was there in the first place.

Then, after more time went by, he found the anger had become a habit. Most days he forgot why he was so angry with her; he only knew that he was. And he knew his anger was justified, very, very justified.

But right now none of that comforted him. For the first time he found himself wishing he could undo everything that had been done the last two years. He wished he and Sam were still friends. He wished she was still the little guy whose company had been so easy that Josh sometimes forgot she was there. He wished she would stop filling his mind with images of her in that blasted, pretty dress. How could he be angry with this new Sam the way he had been angry at the old one? Comparing Sam the way she was now to the way she was then was like apples and oranges. It made him confused to try. And confusion made him angry.

He threw off his covers with a sigh of frustration, dressed for the day, and stormed out of his bedroom. Then he stopped short in the kitchen at the sight of Sam sitting at the table, reading a magazine in her pajamas. When she looked up, she looked as startled to see him.

"I thought you would be gone by now," she said guiltily.

"I got a late start this morning," he said as he sank wearily into the chair across from her.

"Want me to make you some breakfast?" she offered.

Yes. "No." He sipped his coffee and she returned to the magazine. He studied the top of her head, thinking she was a pretty sight first thing in the morning. "What are you reading?"

She held up the intellectual-looking magazine. The cover spouted something about a famine in Africa and its effect on oil prices. Josh waited until she returned to her magazine to smile. Somehow, it was comforting that she still had the same taste in reading material.

"I thought maybe you would read fashion magazines now," he commented.

She looked up questioningly. "Why?"

He shrugged. "Because you're a girl now."

"I was a girl then."

"Not that I recall," he said, his temper starting to simmer.

"I guess you're right," she said tentatively. "I tried hard to act like a man. I had to be careful not to do or say anything to give myself away."

His lips pressed together in an angry line. In retrospect, when he had viewed her life with the knowledge that she was female, the truth had been glaringly obvious. Being so close to her and missing that most important piece of information made him feel like a fool.

"You did a lot to give yourself away if I had been smart enough to pay attention," Josh bit off.

"I was out of context," Sam said. "When something is out of context, such as a woman pretending to be a man, the façade is more believable because there's nothing to compare it to. There have been several psychological studies done on the subject of how context affects object recognition."

Josh's anger increased a notch. "Is that what it was? Were you doing some sort of study on us?"

"Of course not," Sam said. "I was…"

Josh held up a hand to cut her off. "I don't care. I don't care what sick and twisted game you were playing. I don't care what you're doing here now. I think we'll both be better off if we can stay out of each other's way."

Sam looked up at him, debating about how to react. She was at war with herself; the new, independent Samantha she was trying to be wanted to shout at him to stay out of *her* way, thank you very much. But shouting at Josh felt foreign to her, especially when she knew she deserved his censure. She had hurt him; she had to remember that.

"I'll do my best to keep out of your way," she said at last.

Her ready agreement only served to anger him further. "Stop sounding like a whipped puppy all the time."

"Then stop yelling at me all the time," she yelled. His eyes widened in surprise. She set down her coffee with a thump, sloshing some over the side. "I didn't ask to come here, Josh. I'm here at your family's invitation and I have a job to do. I'm not here to make your life miserable. This is a big ranch; I'm sure we can find our own space without bumping into each other at every turn. But on the occasions when we do, stop making it sound like I'm plotting each encounter like a scene from a bad movie." She frowned at him and crossed her arms over her chest. *There. Take that.*

To her further consternation, he smiled. "All right." He downed his coffee in one gulp, rinsed the mug, and set it in the sink before exiting the kitchen. Now that was more like the Sam he had known. He, no, she, had never let him get away with condescension or superiority. In her quiet way, she had always stood up to him and held her own. It had been one of the things he most appreciated about her. But the last couple of years whenever he ran into her, she had seemed like a ghost of her former self. He hated to admit how relieved he was to see some of the old Sam again. Now if only she would ugly up a little bit, everything would be okay. He tried and failed to erase the image of her in her worn, plaid flannel pajamas, her hair slightly sleep-mussed, and her eyes still groggy.

It's a big ranch, he reminded himself, repeating her words. The trick was to find his own space and stay far away from her. He saddled his horse, ready to begin his work for the day, not realizing as he did so that he stared longingly at the house the whole time.

* * *

THE NEXT MORNING they accidentally ate breakfast together again. Josh thought he could avoid Sam by getting up before the sun rose, but he forgot to take New York's time difference into account. In New York, Belle began her day at eight, which meant that Sam began hers at six in Montana. Her day didn't end until six that night when Belle finally left her office at eight PM New York time.

Wearily, Sam took off her headset and rubbed her fingers to her temples. When Belle first described the job, Sam thought she would answer the occasional stray phone call and do some typing. She had no idea she would become an integral part of Belle's team, working closely with her New York secretary, Ethan.

At first Ethan had seemed frustrated with her because she couldn't keep up, but when he found out it was her first day, he had turned helpful and comforting, patiently walking her through whatever information she was missing. By the end of the day, they were beginning to work cohesively, but Sam was drained from all the hard work and anxiety.

She rotated her shoulders, trying to work out the kinks. Outside, a horse nickered. She wondered if it was Ivy's stallion and had the sudden desire to go check. Previously when they were getting along, Josh had teased her about her habit of personifying animals. It was a habit she had picked up as a lonely little girl when animals were her only friends. Now she was twenty and animals were still her only friends.

Pathetic, she told herself. But she still felt cheerful as she stepped onto the porch and sucked a lungful of clean air. Over the years, she had traveled to several large cities with the rodeo, but there was nowhere but the country for her. She liked the clean air and wide open spaces.

Her heartbeat quickened when she saw the stallion standing at his fence, staring at her. Had he actually been waiting for her and attempting to beckon her with his whinny? It certainly seemed that way because as she drew near him he began to prance around his stall importantly, as if trying to impress her. She laughed at his antics and stood on her toes to reach his ear when he came close enough to touch. As before, he closed his eyes and tilted his head toward her, his expression one of utter ecstasy.

"Looks like you've found a friend." Tanner came to stand beside her, his elbows leaning on the fence. The horse opened his eyes and snorted his displeasure at Tanner's appearance. "And a jealous one at that."

Sam laughed. "Isn't he beautiful? I think Ivy has the best job in the world."

"Why aren't you *her* assistant?" Tanner asked.

"I am, sort of. Technically I work for all the King women. It's just that Belle has more for me to do right now." Ivy had told her she needed a bit of light computer help, but maybe she needed help with the horses, too. Sam would have to ask her. "I miss working with the animals."

"You had a way with them. While the rest of us had to manhandle them to get them to do what we wanted, you could get them to follow you with one gentle command, or a glance from your big blue eyes." He laughed. "Still can't believe we didn't know you were a girl."

"Context," Sam muttered.

"Whatever," Tanner said, not sounding like he cared much one way or the other. "What are your plans for tonight?"

Sam looked up at him in surprise. Tanner was a good seven years older than she. Was he asking her out? "Avoiding Josh," she said before she could think. Then she bit her lip. "Don't tell him I said that."

"I won't," Tanner said. "Last guy who said your name in his presence had a busted lip for a month."

Sam winced.

Tanner hurried on. "Come into town with me and get something to eat. You haven't set foot off the ranch in a week."

She wasn't sure the best way to ask what she needed to ask, so she ended up blurting it out. "Are you asking me for a date?"

"No. You're two years younger than my kid sister, so I'm a little repulsed by the insinuation. I have a girl in town. She's a waitress and if you go to dinner with me, it will give me a good excuse to go see her."

"Okay," she said happily. Oddly she felt no embarrassment over her question and his candid answer. She had no interest in Tanner or anyone else, for that matter. Well, almost no one else.

"Are you ready, or do you need to change?" Tanner asked.

"I'm ready," she said as she followed him to the truck.

CHAPTER 11

From his vantage point in the barn, Josh watched as Sam exited the house. *She looks tired,* he thought, absently wondering how her day of work had gone. He was about to go to her and ask when he saw Tanner approach from her other side. He couldn't hear what they were saying, but the conversation looked intimate. Tanner laughed a few times too many.

I warned her not to flirt with the hands, Josh thought angrily. Although he couldn't pinpoint exactly what in her behavior was flirtatious, he was still irritated by the sight of her talking to Tanner. Whatever Tanner said to her made her smile and then they walked to the truck together and drove away.

Josh stared at the spot they had been, dumbfounded. When had Sam and Tanner become so chummy? Were they dating? Obviously so, or why else would they have gone to town together?

He finished unsaddling his horse with angry, jerky movements that only worked to put his horse in a bad mood, too. There had to be some rule about employees not dating each other, didn't there? If he called Cam and asked him, he would no doubt laugh at him. Nonetheless, Josh was determined to do something about this situation. He couldn't say why he was so angry at the sight of Tanner and Sam together; he just was. And, since he had never needed a reason to be mad at her before, he didn't look too closely for one now.

* * *

Sam, however, was having a lot of fun. Tanner was pleasant company. Even on his worst days, he was friendly and easygoing. Tonight he seemed to be making a special effort to entertain her, and it was working. There was no hint of romance or flirtation from him. On the contrary, he seemed to have set himself up as her big brother, offering her advice on the best way to approach the Kings when she wanted something.

"I can't imagine wanting any more than I've already been given," she told him.

"That's because it's new and overwhelming. But eventually being stuck at the ranch so much will get to you, and so will working six days a week, twelve hours a day. You're a young woman, Sam; it's no good to be cooped up all the time. Don't be shy about asking for time off. Because our employment situation is unique, they don't think of scheduling regular time off. But they're not unreasonable. All you have to do is ask, and they'll give it to you."

Since he was trying to be helpful, she didn't disagree with him. But she had a difficult time imagining a scenario where she would ever need to ask for a day off.

"You've worked for them a long time," she said.

"For seven years, since I was your age. And I'll tell you a secret, if you promise to keep it under your hat. I'm planning to ask for a promotion to foreman."

"But they don't have a foreman," she noted.

"True enough, and it's about time they did. With Cade in the office all day and Cam flying to New York half the time, they're hard-pressed to cover all their bases. Making me foreman would give Josh and Coy a break. One of them always has to be there or the men aren't sure who to turn to. With me as foreman, there would be someone in charge when the brothers are away."

"Why would Josh and Coy go away?"

"Coy already goes away. Sometimes he visits his wife's family in Kentucky, and sometimes they get away for a few days to have some time together. Eventually Josh will marry and want the same sort of time off."

Sam blinked at him in dismay. Josh…married? "Do you think he and Chelsea are getting serious?"

Tanner blew out a breath. "With Josh, who knows? I hope not. I get the feeling the rest of the family doesn't like her but are trying to be nice for Josh's sake." He glanced at Sam. "What's your opinion of her?"

Sam pressed her lips together, clenched her fists, but remained silent.

Tanner grinned. "That bad, huh?"

"Josh doesn't see it. He's blind where she's concerned."

"He's blind all around, if you ask me," Tanner said. "You'd make a much better match for him."

"Me?" Sam blurted, pointing to herself.

"You like ranch work. You fit in with the family. You're able to talk Josh down from one of his angry, serious spells."

"But he hates me," she pointed out.

"Sometimes love and hate are closer together than you think," Tanner said. "Two sides of the same coin, you know? Ambivalence, now that's bad. But to hate someone takes a whole lot of passion."

Sam smiled. "No matter how much time I spend around cowboys, I never get used to hearing them philosophize."

"What else are we supposed to do with so much time in the saddle but think about life?"

"What about you and your girl? Are you serious?"

"If I get the promotion to foreman, I'm going to ask her to marry me."

Sam whistled. "It doesn't get much more serious than that."

"What about you? Are you seeing anyone?"

"No," she answered, her tone clipped. "I have no interest in men or dating."

"Why not?" he asked.

"I just..." She twisted her hands nervously in her lap, trying to think of a way to say it. Finally, she simply blurted the truth. "Men scare me."

Tanner glanced sharply at her. "Did something happen to you?"

She nodded and looked away, not wanting to talk about it any further.

They rode in silence for a few minutes.

"But you're not scared of Josh," Tanner said at last.

"No, I'm not scared of Josh," Sam said. Maybe because she had grown used to him in a non-threatening environment when he thought she was a man. Or maybe because she had learned to trust him over a long period of time. Or maybe it was because she knew that, at his core, he was gentle, kind, and unable to physically hurt her. Whatever the reason, she trusted Josh and had no fear of him. There weren't many men she could say that about.

"Maybe you should be," Tanner said quietly. "Oh, I don't think he would ever physically hurt you. But sometimes emotional pain is worse. Josh hasn't yet matured to the point where he can control his temper or his words. He could give you an emotional wound that might never recover."

I think he already has, Sam thought, although she didn't say it out loud. Agreeing with Tanner felt disloyal to Josh, so she simply remained silent. But she took his words to heart and thought about them for the remainder of their drive. Was Josh capable of hurting her even more than he already had? Yes, she decided, but only if she let him. She needed to be careful where he was concerned, which was an irony unto itself. For the first time in her life, she had found a man she felt physically safe with, but she couldn't trust him with her heart.

They arrived in town and parked at the restaurant. Almost as soon as they entered, a pretty girl Sam didn't know sprang forward with a smile.

"Tanner," she said happily.

"Hey, sweetheart," Tanner said. Sam tried not to laugh over his gooey tone that was so different than the one he used with the men on the ranch. The couple became lost in each other's eyes a few seconds before they remembered her. They turned to look at her together. "This is Sam, the one I was telling you about. Sam, this is my girl, Lizzie."

Lizzie regarded Sam with a smile. "You actually thought she was a man at one point? You need to have your eyes checked." She patted Tanner's bicep.

"In his defense, I wasn't wearing a dress at the time," Sam said. She returned Lizzie's smile. "I'm so pleased to meet you. I have no idea how I haven't met you before now. I thought I knew everyone in town."

"I'm new," Lizzie said. "Tanner and I grew up together in Idaho. I moved here to be near him a couple of months ago." Lizzie led them to a table and provided Sam with a menu. Tanner apparently ate here so much he knew what he wanted already. Sam asked Lizzie what was good and took her recommendation of pot roast.

"She seems very sweet," Sam said after Lizzie went to place their order.

"She is," Tanner agreed.

Sam was glad to see him with someone nice. Tanner was one of those men who was genuinely good, and he deserved to find someone equally as kind. When Lizzie brought their food, she brought a plate and ate with them.

"You would think I wouldn't be hungry working around all this food all day, but I still am," she explained. The three of them made small talk together while they ate. Sam enjoyed watching the couple interact with one another. They had known each other all their lives, but things only turned to romance within the last year. Because they had known each other so long, they had a deep rapport with each other and could usually finish each other's sentences. They were sweet together, but the sight also made Sam feel a little melancholy and very much alone.

"I think I'll pop in to say hello at the drugstore," she said in order to give the two some time alone together. She slid out of the booth and began heading toward the store where she had once worked, but she didn't get far.

"Hey, Sam," a voice called.

Sam tried hard to school her features into a placid expression, betraying none of the fear she felt. "Hi, Leo," she said. Leo Tremain stood leaning against the edge of a building. He had the bad habit of appearing from thin air wherever Sam happened to be. Sam was uncomfortable with him, but she was unable to say whether her fear was warranted or simply her standard reaction to all men.

"You're looking good," he said, taking note of her new clothes by sweeping his glance up and down her body.

She swallowed hard and fought the urge to flee. "Thank you."

He left his post on the wall and meandered toward her. "How's life with all those fancy Kings?"

Leo had a long-standing dislike of the King brothers. Sam had no idea why unless it was because his sister, Bet, used to date Cade. But that had been years ago, and they hadn't been serious. And, from what Sam could tell, Leo and Bet weren't close anyway.

"Good so far. They're being very nice to me."

"I'll bet they are," Leo said. She had no idea what his insinuating tone was supposed to mean, but she disliked it nonetheless. After advancing on her with a snail's pace, he at last reached her and stopped short in front of her. "What do you say we go out this Saturday? I'll even make the drive all the way out there to pick you up."

"Um, that's really sweet of you to offer, Leo, but I'm sort of busy right now with my new job."

"So when's a good time?" Leo asked, undaunted. He was good-looking in a swarthy sort of way, but he reminded her too much of the men her mother used to date to ever be attractive to Sam.

"Um, the truth is, Leo, that I'm not really interested in dating anyone right now. Thank you for the offer." She slipped by him and continued on her way to the drugstore, her hands and knees shaking with the effort it took not to sprint away from Leo.

Leo watched her go, his eyes narrowed with resentment. For the last two years he had watched that little slip of a girl with growing interest. She wasn't his usual type, but there was something about her he couldn't let go. What was that word he had heard the other day?

Pristine, that was it. Sam was *pristine.* There was something remote about her that made Leo want to be the one to break through her aloofness. Not that he wanted to keep her around once he did so, but she presented a challenge, and he had always liked a challenge. He had finally made the decision to ask her out when he heard the Kings snatched her up and took her off to their ranch.

His fists clenched in rage. When would the Kings stop thinking the world belonged to them? It wasn't enough that they had the largest and most profitable ranch around. Not enough that they had ruled their high school, taking all the starting positions and leaving talented players like himself on the sidelines. Then they had to go and marry three beautiful women, as if to rub it in the town's faces that they could have whatever they wanted. And now they had Sam. And apparently she now thought she was too good for him, like the Kings.

Someday somebody was going to teach the Kings a lesson, and when they did, Leo would give them a standing ovation.

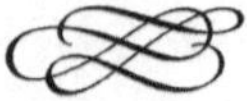

CHAPTER 12

The next day, Sam's job went better than expected. She and Ethan were already developing a flow, learning what the other needed without asking. He confessed that he had been skeptical when Belle hired a Montana secretary, but already Sam was lightening his workload.

Feeling as if she had accomplished something, Sam pulled off her headset with a smile and stood to stretch her aching back. Sometimes she became so task-oriented she forgot to eat. Lunch had come and gone completely unnoticed, and she had only had a cup of coffee for breakfast.

Josh had been noticeably absent at breakfast, and Sam had missed him. Even though they hadn't talked the last two mornings, Sam had enjoyed the quiet intimacy of sharing the meal together. Maybe he was working extra because Cam was gone, she reasoned, and had gotten an earlier than usual start. If that were the case, he was sure to be exhausted. As a way of extending an olive branch to him, she decided to cook a nice meal and invite him to share it.

Her steps slowed as she reached the kitchen, however. There were voices, and one of them was unrecognizable to her. Even worse, it was a woman. With a sinking heart, Sam poked her head around the door of the kitchen and saw Chelsea and Josh standing at the sink, their backs to her. Josh had his hand on the back of her neck in a chaste, yet intimate, clasp. Before Sam could back away slowly, her empty stomach growled, alerting the occupants of the room to her presence. They spun as one and pinned her with a stare.

"What are you doing here?" Chelsea asked, her tone hostile.

Sam looked questioningly at Josh. Hadn't he told her about the new arrangement? If not, how had she missed the latest town gossip? When Josh made no move to answer, Sam took another step into the room.

"I live here." *What are you doing here?* she wanted to retort, but that would be rude.

"You what?" Chelsea snapped, looking to Josh for an explanation.

"My sisters-in-law hired her to be their secretary."

Chelsea crossed her arms over her chest and stuck out her lip in a pout. "Why didn't they hire *me*? I'm your girlfriend, and I hate my job."

"I really can't say," Josh said. "It was their decision." His tone made it apparent he wasn't happy with the situation, either, and that worked to mollify Chelsea slightly.

Maybe it's because none of them like you, Sam thought, smiling sweetly despite such a malicious mental jab.

Chelsea turned her attention back to Sam and noticed her smile with a rush of seething hatred. She felt smug in the knowledge she was one of only a handful of people who had been suspicious of her when she had been posing as a cowboy. She knew there was something not right, although she didn't know what it was. But then Sam had been uncovered as a fraud, and everyone had forgiven her for the deception, thinking what a poor little waste of space she was. Everyone but Josh, that was. Score one for him.

"Why don't you wipe that smug smile off your face and stop acting like you own the place. You're an employee. Make us supper," Chelsea commanded.

Josh frowned and looked between the two women. Chelsea was supposed to irritate Sam, and not the other way around. Sam looked like she couldn't care less that Chelsea was here, and Josh had never seen Chelsea so openly hostile. He was uncomfortable with the display.

"She's not our cook," Josh said evenly.

Sam, who had never been a confrontational person, ignored them both by searching the cupboards until she located a box of cereal. She poured herself a heaping bowl, added milk, and walked to her room, leaving the loving couple bickering behind her. She wondered if it was their first argument.

"I can't believe you didn't tell me about this," Chelsea hissed as Sam walked out of the room.

"I tried," Josh said. "You had to go take care of your grandma."

At first she had no idea what he was talking about, then she remembered her ruse from a few days ago. "You couldn't have called to tell me?"

Josh shrugged. "What's the big deal?"

"What's the big deal?" she echoed furiously. "You're living here in the middle of nowhere with another woman."

"It's not another woman; it's Sam. You know how I feel about her."

"I know you two used to be pretty close." She also knew Sam was pretty in an annoying kind of way. She wasn't an obvious beauty. It was subtle and classic, making her appear unreachable and waiflike, as if she needed to be caught and then protected. She saw the way men looked at Sam, as if she were some rare treasure they needed for their collection. Chelsea knew plenty of men looked at her, too, but not in the same way. Plus, it was annoying that Sam should take any attention at all, especially since she was such a little oddball, always with her nose in a book or talking to some animal. More than once, Chelsea had observed her feeding some stupid stray mutt scraps from her lunch outside the drugstore.

"We were close once. That was then; this is now. Believe me, I want her gone as much as you do."

She believed his sincere tone, but for good measure, she worked up a few tears. "I don't want to lose you, Josh."

Chelsea's tears, which usually worked to wipe away any irritation on Josh's part, didn't have the same effect today. For the first time, he was suspicious of her apparent ability to conjure tears whenever she wanted to end an argument in her favor. Then he immediately felt terrible for his suspicions. This was Chelsea; she was sweet and good and her emotions were close to the surface.

"You're not going to lose me," he said soothingly, drawing her into his embrace. "This situation is temporary until my family feels like they've made up for whatever they think they did in the first place."

With her face pressed to his chest, Chelsea smiled in triumph. *Like shooting fish in a barrel,* she thought. All she ever had to do was turn on the waterworks, and Josh was putty in her hands. Of all the guys she had dated, he was the easiest to manipulate, which was sort of funny because he had a reputation of being hard-nosed. But Chelsea had immediately realized he was soft-hearted if you knew how to push his buttons. And Chelsea definitely knew how to push his buttons. She slipped her arms around his waist, feeling very secure in her control over him, despite her lingering irritation over the girl down the hall.

Above her head, Josh frowned. His thoughts had moved on from the tiff with Chelsea and he was thinking of Sam. She had grabbed a bowl of cereal for supper. In the last few days, he noticed she still wasn't eating enough. She had never eaten enough to keep a bird alive, and she looked even smaller than she had two years ago. Also, had she been limping when she walked to her room? The doctor said she wouldn't have any lingering problems after the accident, but Josh wasn't so sure. He had an impulse to let go of Chelsea and go check on Sam. Was she hungry? Was she in pain? Then Chelsea slipped her arms around his waist and his attention returned to her.

Sam wasn't his responsibility; Chelsea was. With effort, he pushed thoughts of Sam from his mind and concentrated on the girl in his arms.

* * *

THE NEXT MORNING, Sam was surprised to see Josh already sitting at the table. She had risen early because she fell asleep early the night before, but Josh looked like he had been up for a long time already. And he was frowning at her.

She poured herself a cup of coffee, intending to escape to the office, but Josh stopped her.

"Eat something," he said, startling her so that her coffee sloshed over the side of her mug when she jumped.

"What?" she asked.

"You have to eat something. You're wasting away to nothing. What's wrong with you? Why don't you like food?" He rose as he spoke and began pulling food and bowls from the cupboard.

She sank into a chair and watched, dazed, as he prepared a tray of food for her and set it before her. "I don't eat much. You know that." Belatedly, she wondered if she shouldn't remind him that they had previously been close, but he surprised her by smiling.

"I do remember, actually. But that doesn't explain why. Is there something wrong with you?" He sat beside her, pushed the tray of food at her, and scowled.

"There's nothing wrong with me. I'm small and I forget to eat when I get stressed."

"You must be stressed a lot," he said, eyeing her tiny size. He would be surprised if she weighed a hundred pounds.

She shrugged and looked at the food he had set before her. "This is very nice, but I can't eat all this."

"Do your best," he said. He reached across the tray and picked up her sausage biscuit. The sight of her picking at her food brought back old memories from the many meals they had shared together, and it also reminded him that she didn't like sausage.

She drank the juice, poured the milk over her cereal, and ate the banana all while he watched, studying her intently as she chewed. Had it been anyone else, she would have been too intimidated to eat, but she was used to Josh, even when he was in one of his dark moods and not saying a word.

"Does your hip still bother you?" he asked after she finished her food and sat sipping her coffee.

"Sometimes," she said, unwilling to tell him how often it pained her.

"Were you limping yesterday?" he asked, reaching for the last two bites of banana she had left unfinished.

Sam didn't know what surprised her more; the fact that he noticed that she had been in pain yesterday, or that he was eating her leftovers without conscious thought.

"I've been wearing new shoes. They take some getting used to."

"So your feet hurt, and not your hip," he said. He was already leaning forward, but he leaned closer and touched his index finger to her hip. Both of them froze, startled by the action. He hastily withdrew his hand and sat back, but the sensation of his fingertip pressing into her hip lingered.

"It was a combination of both," she said, striving for and failing to find a casual tone. "I should get started." Hastily, she poured another mug of coffee and turned to exit the kitchen. Josh had been mute and frozen since he touched her, so she was surprised when he spoke just as she stepped out of the room.

"Eat with me tonight."

"Why?" For some reason, she didn't turn around. She didn't want to see what might be written on his face in case he was once again shocked by his own actions.

"Because someone has to make sure you're eating," he said.

"Will she be here?" *She* being Chelsea, of course.

"No. She's busy."

Sam nodded. "All right. I'll cook."

"You cook?" he asked, sounding shocked.

She smiled. "You don't know everything about me, Joshua." With that, she walked down the hall to the office, leaving Josh staring at her retreating back.

CHAPTER 13

Sam was right; Josh didn't know everything about her. Namely that she was a good cook. Somehow, she made Tex-Mex food from the ingredients they had on hand already. She tried to explain the combination of staple ingredients she had used, but Josh didn't pay attention. He watched in fascination as she made flour tortillas from scratch and grilled beef, peppers, and onions for fajitas.

"Where did you learn to cook like this?" he asked.

"The rodeo," she said.

"Your stepfather?" he asked.

She grimaced. "No. My mother was in the rodeo since before my birth. The rodeo was where I grew up."

"Your mother was *in* the rodeo?"

"My mother was Rosella," she admitted sheepishly.

Josh's mouth went slack with astonishment. He had never been a huge fan of the rodeo, but even he had heard of Rosella. She was so famous that even people who had no idea what a rodeo was had heard of her. She had gained notoriety because she had been featured in a documentary that won an Oscar. The camera had captured her beauty, charisma, and talent. Most people were in agreement she could have made it as an actress in Hollywood, but she had preferred the countrified lifestyle of the rodeo. Not that it had saved her from a tragic death. She had been killed by a drunk driver when she was in her prime.

"You never told me that before," Josh said.

"I was in a couple of scenes in the documentary, although I was tiny. I didn't want you to put two and two together," Sam said softly. Talking about her mother always made her sad. She had been a bright light and a lot of fun, but never a great mother. Her raging insecurity as a woman had forced her to seek male companionship or fame in order to try and fill the void inside her. Sam had been fun for her to play with when she was in the mood. But when she wasn't, she had forced Sam to the sidelines, leaving her to take care of herself.

"Did your mom teach you to cook?" Josh asked. He turned a chair around and straddled it, propping his elbows on the laddered back.

"My mother was like a butterfly, you know? Beautiful to look at, but not a lot of substance. From the time I was little, she shoved me off on other people whenever she could. She was estranged from her own family, so usually I ended up with someone else from the rodeo. For the first few years of my life, a very nice Mexican lady traveled with us. She was the wife of one of the cowboys, and she set herself up as my keeper. She didn't teach me how to cook, but it was because of her that I wanted to learn. Every morning, she made me tortillas and butter for breakfast, and then at lunch we had tortillas and beans. Everything always tasted so good, unlike when my mother heated something from the freezer for me." Her eyes took on a faraway look as she became lost in memories.

"What happened to her, the lady who used to take care of you?"

She jumped to attention and resumed preparing their food. "She moved on. The rodeo is transient. I learned not to get attached to people, places, or things. These last two years have been the longest I've ever lived anywhere in my entire life."

Josh was fascinated. He had only ever left Montana for brief periods of time. What must it be like not to have roots or family? With a jolt, he realized that the ranch and his family were the closest thing Sam had to a family or roots of her own. Begrudgingly, he began to see what his family had meant about rescuing her. She needed someone to care about her. He only wished it didn't have to be them. She was…complex. Josh didn't like complex. He liked, no, needed simplicity in his life.

She assembled a fajita for Josh and set it before him. He stared at it uncertainly. Generally, he was a meat and potatoes type of guy, not given to being adventurous in his choice of food.

"Come on," she cajoled. "I promise you'll like it."

He tasted it to be polite, but soon discovered she was correct. Usually he wasn't a fan of food that had to be assembled or disassembled in order to eat it, but once he got the hang of piling ingredients into the soft, white tortillas, he found the task less burdensome than he thought it would be.

"Maybe you should cook for a living," he suggested.

"In other words, maybe I could do anything but live here and ruin your life?" she said.

"That's not what I meant. It's just that you're still wasting your potential. You could be so much more than you are now, Sam."

"You want to know the truth, Josh?" Sam said. "Those six months I worked here were the happiest of my life."

He would never admit it, but that had been the last time he was truly happy, too. "You could get a job working with animals again. You could be a veterinary assistant."

"I guess," she said, shrugging. There was no way to tell him that it wasn't working with the animals that had made her so happy; it had been working so closely with him. They had been a cohesive team who could talk about anything or remain happily in silence together. Finding someone she worked so well with wouldn't be easy again. While she had made friends at her last job, there hadn't been anyone at the drugstore that she was especially close to, and no one she missed as she had missed Josh.

Josh was having similar nostalgic thoughts. "Want to watch a movie tonight?"

"Okay," she said, so surprised that it came out sounding like a question. "No date tonight?"

"Chelsea's busy. What about you? Tanner's busy?"

"Tanner," she repeated. "Tanner has a girlfriend. She works at the restaurant in town. Her name is Lizzie. She's very nice."

"Oh," Josh said. He had no idea why this news should make him so happy except that it was always good when one of their employees settled down. It made them more reliable workers. "Good for him." They tidied the kitchen together in comfortable silence and went down the hall to the den.

"What are you in the mood for?" he asked.

A quick glance outside showed the weather to be stormy. "Something scary," she said.

Josh smiled at her unexpected answer, glad she hadn't chosen a romance. "You never choose sappy romances," he said. Previously, she had always gone for action flicks.

"Too depressing," she said. "I would rather see zombies kill people, or something more realistic than two people finding lifelong love."

He frowned at her cynical tone. "You don't think it's possible for two people to be in love forever?"

"Sure it is, but not for me," she replied. She had no idea why she was opening up to him about her deepest thoughts and feelings when the peace between them was still tacit at best, but that had always been the way with Josh. For some reason, she trusted him and always ended up baring her soul to him. She wanted to ask him if he believed in lifelong love. She also wanted to know how serious things were with Chelsea, but Chelsea had always been a touchy subject between them, and Sam didn't want to rock the boat when an extended truce seemed to be building.

Josh opened the computer and scanned the list of movies from the internet. "Why do you think you're the one person in the world who can't fall in love and be happy?"

"Because I don't want to end up like my mother, falling for some loser and eating my heart out when he runs around on me."

"So don't marry a loser."

"Those are the only men who ever like me." Her thoughts turned to Leo Tremain. If her mother were Sam's age, Leo would be exactly her type. That fact alone made him off limits. "Men can't be trusted; men will always hurt you," Sam repeated the phrase she had taught herself as a security measure to ward off potential relationships. Whenever she had found herself attracted to some guy, she would repeat the phrase over and over until her feelings went away.

"Not all men are like that," Josh said.

"True," Sam said. She stared at her hands to avoid allowing him to see what she felt for him. Somehow Josh had slipped in under her radar. No amount of warning herself away could work to make her stop caring about him. At least she could take comfort in the fact that her mother would never have been attracted to someone like Josh. Rosella had been repulsed by anyone who had indelible integrity. The more dishonest a man was, the more her mother liked him.

The movie began and Josh sat back with a frown. Sam was always selling herself short, first in her career choices and then in her personal life. Why would she think she would never get married? She was beautiful, sweet, smart, a good cook, and…He broke off when he realized the rapturous direction his thoughts were heading. Chelsea was his girl; he shouldn't be thinking such nice thoughts about someone else.

The opening credits came to an end, but Josh wasn't paying attention. He was trying to compile a similarly complimentary list about Chelsea. Undoubtedly, she was beautiful. In looks as well as personality, she was almost the opposite of Sam. She was blond and tall with brown eyes. Her beauty wasn't unconventional or hidden like Sam's; it was blatant and she wore it well, playing up her best features with makeup. Seemingly she was almost never at a loss for words, didn't like silence, and had no trouble promoting her own agenda. What else did he like about her? She couldn't cook, but he wasn't too worried about that. She would learn eventually. He had never seen her with kids or animals, but he was pretty certain she would be a good mom. Wouldn't she?

Sam would be a great mom, he thought. He could tell by the way she coddled the puppies. Every day since their birth she had slipped into the barn to hold them and talk to them. He loved to hear her cooing and laughing with them as she talked to Nikita like she was a real person, giving her the rundown of her day.

Stop thinking about Sam, he commanded himself. But how could he stop when she was sitting beside him, her big blue eyes rounded with tension as she sat forward, glued to the screen? Where Chelsea was only a few inches shorter than him, Sam was tiny, engendering a feeling of protectiveness. He wanted to offer Chelsea the same protection that he would any woman, but she needed less than most because she gave off the aura of someone who could take care of herself. Sam, on the other hand…

Outside, thunder boomed and Sam jumped. "Maybe this was a bad idea," she said shakily. "This movie is scarier than I thought it would be. I wanted to be mildly frightened. Now I'm not sure I'll ever sleep again."

I'm right across the hall, Josh wanted to say. *I wouldn't let anything happen to you.* But he couldn't say that; it was much too intimate for their barely perceptible relationship. Theirs was an odd relationship, he realized. There was too much history between them to make them strangers, and too much baggage to make them friends. So what were they?

"We could turn off the movie," he offered.

"I can't do that. Now I'm interested in it," she said without taking her eyes off the screen. "Don't shoot me in the night if you hear me wandering the halls. There's no way I'm staying in my dark and scary bedroom if I wake up afraid."

"Wear a bell," he said. "That way I'll know it's you and I won't shoot you on accident." He was only half kidding. The family took safety seriously; they had to because they were too far removed from town to depend on law enforcement. There were a lot of high-dollar items on the ranch, and though their town had always been relatively safe, none of the brothers was naive enough to believe nothing bad could ever happen to them. Each of them slept with a loaded gun in his room.

"Maybe I'll go to the office and call Ethan," she muttered. Ethan had told her that sometimes when he couldn't sleep, he came into the office in the middle of the night to get caught up on work. New York was a competitive place, and even secretaries had to go over and above the norm to get ahead.

"Who's Ethan?" Josh asked. The fact that he paused the movie during an especially intense scene showed how little he was paying attention to it.

"He's Belle's New York secretary. He's funny, you'd like him."

"I doubt that," Josh said. "I didn't care for Belle's boyfriend, and he was from New York."

Sam laughed. "Josh, not all people who live in New York are the same."

"Sure they are," Josh said.

She rolled her eyes. "And just because you believe something doesn't make it true."

"Sure it does," he said, grinning.

She gave his shoulder a light shove just as a streak of lightning lit up the sky. A house-shaking boom of thunder soon followed, and the house went dark. Sam gave a yelp of surprise. Reflexively, Josh caught her hand, pinning it to his chest.

"It's okay," he said softly, soothingly.

"Sorry," she apologized. "My nerves are a little frazzled from the movie." Indeed, she sounded shaky.

The darkness had an odd effect on Josh. Forgetting Chelsea or anything else that stood between him and Sam, he had the sudden, overwhelming desire to comfort her until her fear ebbed away.

"Why would you be afraid when you know I'm right here?" he asked. His thumb smoothed over her hand where it was still pressed to his chest and he resettled his position until he was closer to her. Now he was close enough to hear her when she caught her breath and swallowed hard before speaking.

"Why would you protect me? You don't like me," she whispered.

The darkness forced her to lower her guard too, causing her to bring up the taboo issue between them.

"If you're under my roof, you're under my care. You're my responsibility, Sam." His fingers trailed up her arm until they rested on her shoulder, toying with the ends of her hair. "Doesn't anyone ever call you Samantha?"

"Not since my mom died," she said, her breath was coming quicker now, and so was her heartbeat. He could practically feel it thudding against her ribcage. Or maybe it was his own pulse thundering in his ears.

"Josh," she whispered. She moved her other hand so it was also pressing against his chest, as if she were going to push him away.

"Don't," he said. "Don't talk, don't move, just don't." He felt like he was perched on the edge of a precipice. One word or move from her would either send him fleeing from the room or would tip the balance in the other direction until he did something he would regret.

"I can't stay here like this," she whispered, her voice strained. It was torture to be so close to him, touching him, and yet still have a gulf between them. He was so close, and yet still so far, and he wasn't the only one who felt the need to flee for self preservation. "I have to go." She tried to stand, but his hands moved to her waist, cinching her close against him.

"Please don't," he said. "Don't go." His face pressed against her neck and he inhaled deeply like someone who had been underwater for a long time and was getting his first taste of air. His palms were on her back, pressing her close. She slipped her arms around his neck and buried her face in his chest.

Love me, she wanted to say. *Let go and love me the way I love you.*

They clung to each other for a moment that seemed to last forever because the tension between them was so thick. Josh knew if he let go, he would kiss her and he was afraid to take things even farther than they had gone. But at last he was overwhelmed by temptation and desire so, inch by painful inch, he peeled himself away from her until they were face to face, so close not even a piece of paper could have fit between them. The room was dark, but the lightning illuminated her face. Her eyes were closed and her lips were parted, her mouth tilted up to meet his. There was no point in trying to resist anymore; he was going to kiss her.

But as his lips settled softly against hers, a heavy boot step in the hallway caused them to freeze before breaking guiltily apart.

"Josh, Sam, are you in here?" It was Coy. A flicker of light in the hallway alerted them to the fact that he had a flashlight. By the time he stepped through the door, they were sitting at opposite ends of the couch. "The rest of the ranch has power, but this place is dark. I think a breaker must have blown. Since I have a flashlight, I'll go down and check the box for you." When he stopped speaking he noticed their unnatural silence. "You two okay?"

"We're fine," Josh said, mentally chastising himself for not checking the electricity already. He hated having to rely on his brothers for something that should be his responsibility. "Thanks."

"No problem," Coy answered easily. For once, Josh was thankful for his easygoing, carefree nature.

He and Sam sat in heavy silence until the lights flipped on. When Coy returned to the room, they were both staring blankly at the wall in front of them. "You guys having a party?" Coy asked.

"We were watching a movie," Sam said. "But the storm knocked everything out."

"Can't you reboot?" Coy asked.

"Yes," Josh said. "We can reboot." Still, he made no move toward the computer.

"Okay," Coy drawled. "Well, enjoy your movie. Looks like the storm is over now, so hopefully we won't have anymore problems."

"Actually, I think I'll turn in," Sam said. She stood and scooted by Josh, careful not to touch him on her way out of the room.

Coy watched her go and turned back to Josh. "Looks like you two are making some progress."

"Yeah, progress," Josh said. He wiped his hand wearily over his face.

Coy stood in the room a minute longer studying him. He would never understand his saintly little brother. Before he met Ivy, if he had found himself in a darkened room with a girl as pretty as Sam, he would have used the opportunity to kiss her. Not Saint Josh, though. If he knew his little brother, they had probably sung songs from the hymnal until help arrived. *Hopeless,* he thought. *The kid is hopeless.* He shook his head as he walked down the hallway and let himself outside.

CHAPTER 14

For as long as he could remember, Josh had had a crush on Chelsea. She had been his ideal since he first noticed her in the eighth grade, so perfect and polished with her long blond hair and pretty brown eyes. She had been the most popular, most sought after girl at school. Though Josh had the sense that she was interested in him, he had waited years to ask her out. He had never been the kind of guy who wanted to date a lot of girls. In fact, he had only ever planned to date one girl, and she would be the girl he would marry. For that reason, he had held off asking Chelsea out until he was certain she was the girl he wanted.

When he was eighteen, he finally decided it was time to make his move, and then he had learned his best friend was secretly a woman. For a while, he had gone into an emotional tailspin as he hibernated from the world and questioned the reality of everything he knew. By the time he emerged, Chelsea was dating Leo Tremain, a detestable character if ever there was one. The fact that Chelsea dated him for a few months was a blip in her otherwise perfection, but Josh chalked the relationship up to Chelsea's naïve, trusting nature. Someone who was as innocent as she was couldn't possibly understand how inno-cent Leo *wasn't*.

Six months ago, he had finally asked her out. Since he knew she was the girl he was going to marry, they had been serious almost from the beginning of their relationship, spending at least one evening a weekend going on dates. She was the first girl he had ever dated, kissed, or said "I love you" to. He planned for her to be the last girl he did any of those things with. And now he had to break up with her.

His heart was heavy as he drove to town the next day after work. He hoped Chelsea would be home and he wouldn't have to track her down. He should have called, but he didn't want his somber mood to alarm her unnecessarily.

Chelsea wanted to scream in frustration when she opened her door and saw her mopey boyfriend standing on the other side, his expression even more hangdog than usual.

"This is a surprise," she said through clenched teeth. Immediately her mind began constructing an excuse to get out of spending an entire evening trying to cajole him out of whatever sad mood he was in. On the other hand, thinking up excuses to get away from him would come in handy when she lived in the middle of nowhere on his boring ranch. Being set for life was a high price to pay, but for the financial security of being married to a King, Chelsea was willing to do whatever she had to.

"Are you busy?" Josh asked.

"Well, actually I…" she began, but he continued speaking as if he hadn't heard her.

"Because we need to talk."

Chelsea frowned. What could they possibly have to talk about unless he was finally ready to pop the question? But unless he was even stuffier than she gave him credit for, he didn't look like someone who was about to propose. She opened the door wider, granting him access. He plodded behind her to the living room and sat on the couch. She waited for him to speak, but he remained silent. He finally started to ramble. She mentally zoned out, reviewing her list of friends to see which one she was going to unload on about Josh's most recent unannounced appearance when something he said finally caught her attention.

"What did you say?" she asked, focusing her attention sharply on his face.

"I said I think we should break up."

Panic, sudden and intense, overwhelmed her. What had he heard? Who had been talking about what she did behind his back? Why else would he suddenly decide to dump her out of the blue? "Why?" she asked, and she didn't have to feign the shock in her tone.

"Because I'm confused, and I don't think it's right that I should keep you on the string while I try and deal with what's going on inside my head."

"Why are you confused?" she asked. *You big idiot,* she added to mentally. Just when she had him exactly where she wanted him, he decided to go and start thinking about things. Could he be any more annoying?

Josh wasn't sure how to tell her without throwing Sam under the bus, but he also felt the need to be honest. "Since Sam has come back into the picture, things have changed," he said bluntly.

Chelsea's mouth fell. Sam? This was about Sam? Choirboy Josh was cheating on her and dumping her for another woman? She wanted to kill him; she wanted to kill that little runt Sam. Somehow, she would get Josh back, and then she would obliterate the little cross-dressing tramp who had caused all this trouble. Once Chelsea and Josh were married, she would make sure Sam was fired, thrown off the ranch, tarred, feathered, and run out of town. As phase one in her plan, she burst into tears.

"I can't believe you're breaking up with me," she said. To her delight, Josh looked wretched.

"I'm sorry," he said. "I never meant for this to happen, I'm just...confused."

"But why would you be interested in Sam when she's dating Leo?"

Josh froze. "She's what?"

Inwardly, Chelsea seethed at his jealous tone. She wiped her eyes and sniffled pathetically. "She's going out with Leo. He told me so." Actually, what he had told her was that he had asked Sam out and she turned him down. He had also used a few choice words about Sam and Josh before he kissed her in the backseat of his truck the night before.

Instinctively, Josh wanted to recant on his breakup. How could Sam be dating Leo when she had just told him she wasn't interested in anyone? That niggling thought ate at him and kept him from reneging on his breakup. "Leo lies."

"I saw them making out in the backseat of his truck."

Josh frowned, getting angrier and more confused by the second. Something about what she was saying didn't ring true, but Chelsea wasn't a liar. Maybe she had seen someone else. "When?"

She sniffed and looked at him in surprise. He usually swallowed whatever she told him without checking up on her. She thought fast. "Last night." If anyone had seen Leo in the backseat of his truck, it would be easy to insist that it was Sam and get someone to back up her story.

"That proves it wasn't Sam. She was with me."

To his consternation, this only made Chelsea cry harder. "You were cheating on me with her last night?"

"I was not," Josh said vehemently, then flushed guiltily when he remembered their clinging embrace on the couch. Technically he had cheated on her, though probably not to the degree she had in mind.

"But we're happy together," Chelsea said in between her tears. "I love you."

He opened his mouth to say he loved her, too, but the words wouldn't come. What was wrong with him; this was Chelsea, his dream. He did love her, didn't he? Why couldn't he get the words out when he had said them easily before? At least he could agree they had been happy together, couldn't he? He searched his mind, trying to find some happy memories, but right now they were crowded by pictures of her crying any time they disagreed. Without fail, her tears worked to sway him in her favor, effectively ending the argument. He had enjoyed the kissing immensely, but was that enough to base a relationship on?

These new doubts added to his confusion, but they also strengthened his resolve. Maybe breaking up right now was the right thing to do for a number of reasons.

Chelsea wanted to stomp her foot in frustration when crying did nothing to sway Josh. Tears had always worked before; why weren't they working now? Instantly, they dried up, only to be replaced by anger.

"Fine. If you want that little lying schemer, then you're welcome to her. But trust me when I tell you that she's still playing you, Josh. Someday soon you're going to learn the truth about her, and maybe if you're lucky I'll take you back." She turned her back to him and walked out of the room, slamming her bedroom door so hard the pictures in the hallway rattled.

Josh sat frowning at the door, not only because he had never seen Chelsea so angry before, but also because he wasn't altogether sure her words weren't true. Could he trust Sam? Did he want to? Just because he found himself attracted to her didn't mean he wanted to be with her. It was Chelsea who had made that leap. She would probably never believe him, but he wasn't breaking up with her in order to pursue Sam. He was breaking up with her because he had done something wrong and needed to make amends by getting out of a relationship where he had broken trust.

He stood and let himself out of the house wondering why he felt a small sense of relief mixed in with his sadness. Confusion numbed his brain, fogging his thoughts. He wanted Chelsea, didn't he? But he couldn't be with her as long as he was attracted to Sam. He didn't want to be with Sam because he didn't trust her, and he was still angry at her over her deception. Why, then, wasn't he heartbroken over the loss of his girlfriend? Shouldn't he be desolate that he was single instead of speeding toward home to see Sam?

As if she had been waiting for him she ran out of the barn to meet him.

"Josh, Josh, Josh," she called excitedly. She dashed up to him and clasped his hand. "The puppies opened their eyes. You have to come and see." She dragged him behind her to the barn then let him go to throw herself down beside Nikita.

"Look at them, Nikita. Your babies are growing up," she said. Nikita thumped her tail happily and draped her head on Sam's leg as her puppies blinked sleepily and pawed at their mother for a snack. Sam picked up a puppy and beamed at Josh. His heart turned over before thumping a few times and sputtering back to life.

"What's wrong with you?" Sam asked, her smile slipping slightly.

"Did you ever go out with Leo?"

She wrinkled her nose. "Ew, no. He did ask me out when I went to town last week with Tanner, but of course I said no. I would never go out with someone who walks like that."

"Walks like what?" Josh asked.

"He's a sidler. He sneaks up to people like a snake. It's creepy."

Josh laughed and picked up one of the puppies who had startled at the sound. "That's how you select who you'll go out with? By the way he walks?"

"That's part of it. You can tell a lot about a man by the way he walks."

"So what do you look for in a walk?" he asked.

She closed her eyes and pictured him walking. "Determination in each step, like he knows exactly where he's going and why and won't let anything stand in his way."

"What if he actually shoves people out of his way, does that make him even more attractive?"

"Nah, he would never shove people out of his way. They jump aside in fear at the sight of him. He's that cool and intimidating."

"Sounds like you already have someone in mind," Josh said.

She brought the puppy to her face to avoid answering. What good did it do to fantasize over him when he no doubt spent the evening with Chelsea? Sam, on the other hand, had eaten a lonely dinner in front of the computer, finishing the movie they had started the night before.

"Belle and Cam are coming home tomorrow," she blurted for lack of something better to say.

"Why?" Josh said. "They've barely been gone a week."

"Something Cam needs to do, I don't actually remember. Ethan and I were swamped today, and I wasn't paying attention to the reason they're going to be here. It's a quick trip, though. They'll be home for a few days and then they're going back to New York for a month or two."

"You and Ethan sound chummy," he said casually.

"He's been a lifesaver. He's patient with me and helps me out whenever I'm stuck. Not everyone would be so magnanimous."

Josh was suddenly glad this Ethan person was far away in New York. "He's not coming with Cam and Belle is he?"

"No. Why would he come here? I'm here; his job is there. That's the point of having two secretaries. If we ever met face to face, the world would probably implode or something."

"Did you eat?" Josh blurted.

"I had some cereal."

"Sam," he intoned, dropping the puppy gently onto the hay. "Come on." He stood and held out his hand to her.

"Where are you taking me," she asked, allowing him to lead her from the barn.

"I'm feeding you."

"But I already ate."

He threw her a disparaging look over his shoulder. "Cereal is not supper."

"But I'm not hungry," she said.

"I am, and I don't want to eat alone." For the first time in recent memory, he had been too upset to think about food. Now that he was home, however, he was starving. They entered the kitchen and washed their hands. Sam sat at the table and watched while Josh scrambled eggs and made toast. She shouldn't have been surprised when he cracked eight eggs, but she still was.

"Josh, I can't eat all that," she said.

"I can. I've eaten a dozen before, but I think my metabolism is starting to slow."

"Yeah, you're getting a little pudgy," she said.

He turned to look at her over his shoulder, an eggshell frozen in midair. "Am I? Where?"

Since he was six feet of solid muscle, she had no real reply. "I don't want to say; I might hurt your feelings."

He faced the eggs again with a smile that quickly slipped. He shouldn't be smiling on the same night he broke up with his girlfriend, should he? Poor Chelsea was probably crying her eyes out over his betrayal, and he was enjoying himself with Sam. What was wrong with him? What kind of horrible person was he?

"Josh, are you okay?" Sam asked.

Once again, Josh thought of Chelsea. Had she ever asked him that? Had she ever cared what he was feeling or thinking? At the moment he couldn't think of one solitary time she had ever asked him a question about himself. Sam, on the other hand, was seemingly still attuned to his moods and actually cared what he was feeling and thinking.

"I'm fine," he lied. He was anything but fine; he was more confused than he had ever been.

The eggs finished cooking. He divided them between their plates and buttered the toast. Sam ate a few bites and sat watching him devour the food on his plate.

"Sam, you ate exactly three bites," he said accusingly.

"I'm not sure how many bites you ate. I can't count that high."

He rolled his eyes and leaned over the table, loading a bite of eggs onto his fork. "Open," he commanded, shoving his fork toward her mouth. By feeding her, he was able to get her to eat four more bites before she pushed his hand away and shook her head.

"I can't Josh, really. I'm stuffed. Thank you for trying, but I'm not hungry."

"I'm worried about you," he said, surprising both of them. There was a part of him that was still horribly angry with her; how could he be concerned about her wellbeing at the same time?

"I'm fine, really. I eat when I'm hungry."

"But you're never hungry," he said.

"Sometimes I am."

"Eat one more bite," he coaxed.

Stubbornly, she pressed her lips together and shook her head. The sight of her mutinous expression brought out a teasing nature he didn't know he possessed. "You're going to take one more bite, willingly or not," he said. Of course he wouldn't actually force feed her, but he wanted to see her reaction to his threat.

"You can't," she began, but was interrupted by a forkful of eggs stuffed between her lips. He hadn't known he was actually going to shove the food in her mouth until she opened it, but he knew a golden opportunity when he saw it.

Sam sputtered, spitting most of the egg back into his face. "Oh, it's on now," he said. He grabbed a fistful of egg in his bare hand. With a yelp that was half scream, half giggle, Sam stood to her feet and sped down the hallway, Josh close on her heels. She darted into the office and led him in a chase around her chair before sliding over the desk and running back out of the room. With her small size and lithe movements, she had always been quicker than him, a fact that used to gall him when they worked together.

She darted into her room and tried to lock the door, but he pushed it open and stormed into the room, his egg hand held aloft. He smiled triumphantly because he knew he had her cornered, but before he could reach her she darted around him and escaped the room.

The only open door was directly across the hall. Not until she had run into it did she realize it was his room. That was also the same point she realized there was a laundry basket sitting a few feet inside the doorway. She tripped, landing hard on the bed, facedown. Josh plopped down beside her.

"Roll over," he commanded.

She shook her head and hunkered farther into the mattress for protection.

"I guess I'll have to make you," he said. Keeping the egg hand aloft, he used his free arm to try and roll her over, but she wriggled away from him. Finally, he pinned her with his knee like an errant calf and then carefully turned her over, wedging her beneath him.

"Time for some egg," he said, his hand making a slow descent toward her face.

"I'll bite you," she threatened.

"Thanks for the warning. I'll just drop the egg in and keep my hand out of your way."

She twisted her head to the side and that was when they heard it.

"His truck is outside. One of them has to be here." It was Cam.

"Maybe they're in the barn," Belle said.

"This late at night?" Cam asked. "Besides, I thought I heard something from one of the bedrooms."

"Do you think they're asleep already? I was hoping to talk to Sam."

"Honey, let the girl have the night off. She's been working like a dog."

"I wanted to see how she was doing," Belle said.

"And ask if you had any messages since you left New York," Cam added. "Don't try to guilt me; I know you."

Their voices became more distinct as they moved up the hall. Sam and Josh froze, glad they hadn't turned the light on. They were both desperately hoping they wouldn't be discovered. There was no good way to explain why Josh had her pinned to his bed with a wad of egg in his hand. They barely dared to breathe as Belle and Cam walked slowly up and down the hallway, wondering where Sam and Josh could be. Thankfully they didn't think to look inside Josh's darkened room, even though the door was open.

"I thought they weren't coming home until tomorrow," Josh dared to whisper as soon as he was sure they couldn't be heard. Just in case, he moved so his mouth was close to her ear.

"That's what Ethan told me," Sam whispered, shifting so her mouth was close to his ear.

The outside door slammed, indicating Belle and Cam had exited the house. But just in case, Sam and Josh remained frozen to their spots for another moment, each wondering how they had gotten there in the first place. Josh couldn't believe he had actually chased a girl down, intending to stuff egg into her face. Never had he had such a monumental lapse in manners. Sam couldn't believe she had inadvertently wound up squished beside Josh in his bed. Could there be a more awkward place to be found by her new employer? What had she been thinking, running through the house and giggling like a twelve year old?

"Do you think it's safe for me to go now?" she asked.

No. Stay here for the next twelve hours, or s, was his first shocking thought. Instead, he answered rationally. "I think the coast is clear." Still, he made no move to leave.

"You're going to have to get up so I can go. You're squishing me."

That was when he realized he was lying half on top of her; he had thought the blanket was bunched beneath him. He was suddenly glad for the fist full of egg he held; it kept him from reaching for her and pulling her even closer. Instead, he rolled away from her and let her go. After she stood, he shimmied off the bed and followed her to the door. He was so much taller than her they were both able to poke their heads out the door like a bad sitcom where multiple characters peek around the same corner. Since there was no sign of Belle or Cam, she darted across the hall to her room.

Her eyes were downcast as she closed her door, but at the last second, she chanced a glance at him. When he winked at her, he was almost certain she blushed before the soft click of the door echoed down the hall.

CHAPTER 15

The next morning, Cam, Belle, and Josh were already up when Sam arose. She double checked the time, making sure she hadn't mistakenly overslept, but it was only five o'clock, her normal wakeup time.

"Good morning," she said shyly.

"Morning," Cam returned cheerfully.

Belle grunted into her coffee.

"Belle's not a morning person," Cam explained, rubbing his wife's back in a comforting circle. "She'll cheer up after the coffee kicks in."

"Morning," Josh said. "Hungry?" He gave her a wicked smile. She flicked his Stetson as she passed him.

"No, coffee for me," she said. She sat down between Belle and Josh, unconsciously mimicking Belle by sipping her coffee in silence while Cam and Josh talked shop.

"So you flew all the way home to sign a few papers?" Josh asked incredulously. "We could have faxed them to you."

Cam shook his head. "It was tax information. The signatures needed to be original. Plus, Belle wants to take Sam back with us."

This pronouncement was met by stunned silence.

"Back to New York?" Josh asked. "For how long?" Somehow, he

refrained from scooting protectively closer to Sam as he imagined her alone in the big, bad city.

"A couple of days," Cam said. "Belle thought she would appreciate seeing how things operate at the office in New York since they seem to be working together so often."

Belle grunted, possibly in agreement, and took another sip of her coffee.

"When are you leaving?" Josh asked. His eyes darted to Sam. Oddly, his first thought was for Nikita and her puppies. They would be lonely without their daily visit with Sam. And what about Ivy's stallion? The brute had fallen in love with Sam; he would no doubt be heartbroken without glimpsing her daily. And then there was him. Begrudgingly he admitted he would miss her too. The house would seem empty without her. He had no idea how much he had come to depend on seeing her smiling face first thing in the morning or late at night when he finished work.

"Today," Cam said. "As soon as I finish up my work here. If that's okay with Sam, of course."

All eyes turned to Sam. "Sure," she said, then bit her lip. "Except I don't have any luggage." She blushed as she imagined loading her pretty new clothes into garbage bags and dragging them to the airport.

"Yes you do," Belle said groggily. "They're in the hall closet. Did we forget to tell you we bought you some luggage?"

"Oh," Sam said. She would never get used to the overwhelming mixture of emotions she felt whenever the family heaped generosity on her. How could she ever repay all that they had done for her?

Belle, sensing her dismay, hurried to change the subject. "Ethan is dying to meet you. I think maybe he's already half in love with you, and he hasn't even seen you yet."

Sam laughed. After a few days of working together she realized that Ethan was a shameless flirt who probably hit on anything that moved. Still, she was curious about the voice on the phone. He had been very nice to her, and she wanted to thank him in person for his help.

"I'm going with you."

Now everyone's head swiveled to Josh as he made his pronouncement. "You? New York?" Sam asked, incredulous. Josh was one of those people who believed New York was the birthplace of original sin.

Across from her, Cam sputtered a laugh and choked on his coffee.

"I should probably see where Cam and Belle live when they're not here," Josh said.

"Um, Josh, you're more than welcome to come with us, you know that, but don't get excited about our apartment. It's the size of this room," Belle said. "I think you'll like New York, though." She adored Manhattan and couldn't imagine anyone who didn't feel the same.

"Sure," Josh said unconvincingly. He had no plans to step outside their apartment, except to accompany Sam to Belle's office, of course. He didn't like the sound of this Ethan character.

"If you're coming with us, we have even more work to do before we're ready to go," Cam said, standing. He leaned down to kiss Belle. "Don't work Sam so hard she doesn't have time to pack."

"We'll pack first, then I can wring every last drop of work out of her until we have to leave," Belle said, tipping her face up to return his kiss.

"Good luck, Sam," Cam said, throwing her a sympathetic look. "Better have another cup of that coffee. See you ladies in a few hours." He jammed his Stetson on his head. Josh stood to follow him. He looked as if he wanted to say something, but couldn't with Belle sitting there. Instead, he grabbed his hat and followed his brother from the house.

As soon as the men were clear of the room, Belle started talking. And she didn't stop for the next five hours.

First, she hustled Sam off to her room and told her which clothes would be New York appropriate. Sam appreciated the help because she had no idea what to wear. After packing, which took a record ten minutes under Belle's tutelage, Belle began working.

If Sam had thought her new job was hectic with Belle a dozen states away, she was completely unprepared for what it was like to work with Belle in the room. The woman was an endless swirl of activity. Her mind seemed to go in ten different directions at once, and she never lost track of what she was doing. Simultaneously, she held three different conversations on three different lines while she reviewed two contracts and typed an email. Sam had never seen anything like her.

She kept up, which made her feel immensely proud of herself, but she was exhausted. If this was what Ethan's life was like every day, it was no wonder he often worked in the middle of the night. It was probably the only time he could get a moment's peace or get caught up on all the work Belle required.

When the men returned home and announced it was time to leave, Sam wanted to weep with joy. Her legs were shaking from running around the tiny room and bending down to retrieve folders. For once, she was starving so when Josh asked her if she was hungry, she practically fell on him in her enthusiasm to get her answer out.

"Yes, oh please yes, can we eat?"

He laughed at the sight of her clasped hands and big eyes, practically begging for food. "You look like Oliver Twist," he said.

"I'm an orphan, but not a pickpocket," she answered.

"Belle, come on, honey. Time for food," Cam said.

"One more minute," Belle called absently, her attention still solely focused on the computer in front of her. Cam rolled his eyes, grabbed the back of the wheeled office chair she was sitting in, and pulled her down the hall toward the kitchen. Once away from her computer, she either sat back and enjoyed the ride or realized fighting her husband was useless and gave in.

They ate a hurried lunch of sandwiches together. Josh excused himself to throw some things in a bag, and then they were off. One of their hands drove them to the small airstrip in town where their jet was waiting.

When they were first married, Cam had intended to get his pilot's license and buy a small plane. Then he realized that he had no time to get his license, let alone attain all the instrument ratings he would need in order to accomplish a cross-country flight. Along with that, there were all the logistical problems of how to keep and maintain an airplane on the ranch. In the end, he and Belle joined a co-op with a few other families and held joint shares in a leer jet. It was faster and roomier than an airplane would have been, and, better yet, they didn't have to do any of the maintenance or upkeep. Since they usually flew in the middle of the week, they rarely ran into scheduling conflicts with the other families who generally only used the plane to fly to vacations.

Josh had no idea how Cam and Belle could afford such a luxury, but Cade did the books, and he assured Josh his brother was fine. There was always something cryptic in Cade's tone, as if he knew something Josh didn't, but Josh couldn't figure out what it was. Maybe it was simply that Belle made a whole lot more than Cam. If so, there was good reason Cam kept the information to himself. No reasonable man wanted to think his wife made more than he did, at least Josh wouldn't like that. He intended to be the breadwinner in his family.

Josh's resolve held out until they boarded the jet, and then fear began to settle in. He had never flown before. Now he was making his debut in an airliner that was practically the size of one of their draft horses. To be sure, it was comfortable-looking with its leather interior and wood trim, but to Josh it looked like a coffin with wings.

Cam told them where to stow their baggage. He and Belle took the seats in the front behind the pilot, leaving the two back seats for Josh and Sam.

Sam was so excited, she could hardly hold still. Perhaps it wasn't dignified to flit around and wiggle like one of Nikita's puppies, but that was what she felt like doing. Somehow, she refrained, but it took a lot of effort to try and look unaffected by her new adventure.

She sat and buckled herself in. The engine started, and they began rolling down the runway. She smiled at Josh but quickly realized he wasn't sharing in her excitement. His hands were white-knuckling the seat, his eyes were squeezed tightly shut, and his face looked a little green.

"Josh." She had to say his name twice before he opened his eyes.

"What do you think about Congress's latest plan for the FDA to track livestock?"

It took a couple of seconds for the incendiary question to register, then he let go of the seat and leaned forward, his face red with anger.

"I think it's a bunch of bull, no pun intended. If they want to sound the death knell for the beef industry, then they should go ahead, but…" And on and on he went for the next half hour until the jet was safely in the air and flying smoothly. When at last he finished his tirade, he was surprised to see the aircraft sailing gently over the clouds. He blinked, amazed he had survived takeoff. What had happened to his anxiety? How had it dissolved so quickly? *Sam.*

She smiled at him as she guessed the direction of his thoughts.

"Do you really care about the FDA's plan to track livestock?" he asked, somewhat chagrined at how easily she had handled him.

"You know I do," she said sincerely.

He returned her smile because he believed her. She did care about the things that affected the ranch, and she was well educated on the topic. He could talk to her as well as any man on the subject, which was a nice change. Chelsea hadn't even pretended interest when he talked about things that affected the ranch. For the remainder of the flight, they talked politics. After a while, Sam told him about some of the situations she had been tracking in the Middle East. Somehow, she made things interesting for him so that he found himself riveted, realizing for the first time how everything in the world affected his little corner of Montana in some way.

All too soon, they were in New York. Actually, according to Belle, they were in New Jersey. The airports in New York were too large to accommodate their small jet, so they landed in New Jersey and took a car into the city.

It was another hour and a half to drive into the city. Josh stared out the window and had all his worst fears confirmed—the place was a dirty slum. Trash piled on sidewalks, graffiti lined buildings, and homeless people panhandled practically on every corner. Why would anyone willingly live here? It was horrible, like a scene from a post-apocalyptic movie. Everything everywhere was a study in despair.

Finally, when he couldn't take it anymore, he closed his eyes and rested his head on the seat behind him.

Sam sighed in exasperation as she watched Josh. Granted the neighborhoods near the airport were not pretty. But the closer they drew to Manhattan, the more picturesque and upscale everything became. And Josh was missing all of it. He was a small-town guy who loved his life in Montana. Most of the time, she appreciated the fact that he was perfectly content with his life. But there were other times, like now, that she wanted to shake him for his narrow-minded approach to life. Somehow, she would have to find a way to open his eyes to his surroundings and get him to take a walk on the wild side.

With the time difference, it was late by the time they arrived at Cam and Belle's apartment. Sam was enthralled with the building. It was an authentic brownstone, like she had always seen on television, and they had a real, live doorman. He opened the door and tipped his hat politely to her, even though she stared at him like he was a foreign creature in a zoo.

Josh was morose and homesick, a combination which made him irritable, so he wisely remained silent. Belle hadn't been kidding when she said their apartment was tiny. There was one bedroom and barely enough room in the living room for him to stretch out his legs on the floor. Sam took the couch but because the room was so tiny, they were in touching distance of each other.

For that reason, it shouldn't have been a surprise when she touched him, but it still was.

"What do you want to do tomorrow?" she asked, laying her hand gently on his shoulder from her loftier position on the couch.

"I suppose we'll have to see Belle's office." *And meet this Ethan person.*

"But after that. Belle said I can have the day off tomorrow after I tour the office with her."

"Come back here, I suppose."

Sam sighed and squeezed his shoulder. "Come on, Josh, we're in the greatest city in the world. Think. What are things you've seen on television that you would like to see in person?"

Absently, he caught her hand in his and smoothed his thumb over her palm while he thought. "I'd like to see that giant bull statue near Wall Street." With anyone else, he might be too shy to make such a request, but Sam wouldn't judge him for his lack of ambition.

"I'd like to see that, too," Sam said. "Anything else?"

"I'd like to see where the towers fell on 9/11."

"That's sort of depressing. I'm going to need something cheery to counterbalance it," she said.

He smiled, pressing her palm to his lips. "Central Park?" he suggested.

"Perfect," she said.

"What do you want to see?" he asked.

"Rockefeller Center."

They lay in silence a few minutes. "Do you think it's safe?" he asked. "Maybe we should stick with one of those guided tours."

"Josh, did you notice the way people dress here? You're the only six-foot tall cowboy with leather boots and a Stetson in all of Manhattan. You're the freak here. You wrestle huge bulls as part of your daily job, and when you use a gun you have the aim of a professional sharpshooter. I'm fairly certain we're safe because no one in his right mind would even think of attacking you." She pressed her palm to his cheek and felt him smile again.

"I guess I never thought of it that way," he said. Strangely, he was suddenly looking forward to the day tomorrow. The thought of trekking through the huge city on their own was beginning to sound like an adventure. He began to think of it the same way he had thought of trekking through the Montana wilderness when he was a kid. *Bring it on,* was his last drowsy thought before he fell asleep.

CHAPTER 16

The next morning, Cam and Belle took them out for breakfast. Josh had to admit the food was good. While Belle buzzed excitedly about the city, Cam sat back, smiling at his wife. Josh thought his devotion to New York wasn't as hearty as Belle's but he still seemed to enjoy it. He looked at ease and at home here, which was strange and disconcerting to Josh. He was used to seeing his brother in charge of their ranch. Seeing him in a pair of khaki pants and a polo shirt sipping coffee in some tony Manhattan eatery was like watching another person.

Next they went to Belle's office. Josh didn't think it was his imagination that people cleared a path for her as soon as she walked in the door. It was strange; Belle wasn't mean, but people were still afraid of her. She was also different here. Gone was the klutzy uncertainty of Montana. Here she walked with purpose on heels that looked impossibly high. People stopped to look at her in deference, the same way the ranch hands in Montana looked at Cam.

She led Sam through the office, pointing out different people Sam had apparently worked with over the last few days. Josh had no idea if Sam was taking it all in; he was certainly confused and overwhelmed.

At last they stopped at a large office with Belle's name on it. In front of the office was a desk, and behind the desk sat a man who stood and smiled at the sight of their group. Belle turned toward the man and presented Sam with a flourish.

"Ethan, this is Sam; Sam, this is Ethan."

"The Montana me," Ethan said. Taking her hand, he kissed it and bowed. Josh tried to size him up. He wasn't the prissy sissy he had been hoping for. He looked more masculine than a male secretary should. Maybe the term secretary was a misnomer because, from what Josh had heard, the guy was more like an executive assistant.

"And this is my brother-in-law, Josh," Belle introduced. Ethan dropped Sam's hand, leaving his hand free to extend toward Josh.

"Hi," he said, sounding friendly.

"Hello," Josh said. He probably sounded a little less than friendly as he continued to try and size Ethan up. Unknowingly, he took a step closer to Sam, but stopped himself from putting his arm around her. That would be awkward since they weren't actually together. Still, he felt protective of her. Despite her apparent comfort with the city, she was a small-town country girl.

"So you're Cam's brother," Ethan said. "I've been curious about you guys. It's nice to finally meet one of you."

Josh had no idea why he, Coy, or Cade should be of interest to Ethan. Why would he take such interest in his boss's brothers-in-law? Belle shot Ethan a quelling look. "Ethan is curious about all things Montana," she said. Again, Josh didn't understand her warning tone. He hated feeling like he was missing something.

"One of our authors writes about Montana a lot," Ethan explained. "It's made me curious. And of course it's where Belle and Cam are from."

"Who writes about Montana?" Sam asked.

"Suzanne Rey," Ethan replied.

"Oh, right," Sam said. The author's second best seller had been on the list for over a month. "I didn't know this firm represented her."

"I represent her," Belle said.

"I love her work," Sam said. If she lived in Montana and Belle represented her, maybe there was a chance she might get to meet her.

"She's very reclusive and private," Belle said, guessing her thoughts. "She doesn't do signings or make public appearances. Ever."

"She doesn't even have a picture in the back of her books," Ethan added with a smile.

"Enough," Belle said. She handed Sam off to Ethan and instructed him to show her how things work. There was nothing for Josh to do but watch helplessly as he whisked her away. "Want to wait in my office, Josh? It shouldn't take too long, unless Ethan gets chatty. Then she could be here all day."

Josh followed Belle to her cushy office and sank into a plush leather sofa.

"So I take it he's not married?" Josh said.

"Hmm," Belle had already begun to concentrate on her work for the day and had no idea what he was talking about.

"Ethan. Is he married?"

"He's only twenty-seven," Belle said absently, staring at her computer.

"You're only twenty-four," he reminded her.

"Yes, but I'm the exception to the rule on several counts," she said.

That was certainly true; she and Cam both seemed much older than they were.

"Wait, are you jealous?" Belle asked.

"No, it's just that Sam is innocent," Josh said.

"You don't have to worry about Ethan. He's a nice guy."

Josh scowled at the coffee table in front of him. That wasn't the reassurance he had been looking for. After what felt like forever, Sam and Ethan returned to the office, laughing and talking like they had known each other forever. The sight of her being so carefree with another man made pain knife through his midsection and he realized with a start that he *was* jealous. How could he be jealous of someone he still wanted to keep his emotional distance from?

"Ready?" Sam asked. When she smiled, all his raging inner turmoil died away and he smiled in return.

"As I'll ever be," Josh said.

"Let me know if you guys get bored later," Ethan said. "My offer still stands. I'll show you the sights."

"Thanks, Ethan," Sam said. "Thanks for the time off, Belle."

"Have fun," Belle called from inside her office.

"So, with Ethan's help, I sort of mapped out our route today so we don't have to do a lot of backtracking."

"What do you mean with his help?" Josh asked suspiciously.

"I mean I asked a guy who lives here the best way to see everything we want to see without backtracking. In Montana we call it asking for directions," she said. "What's wrong with you?"

"Nothing," Josh said, trying hard to pull himself out of his dark mood. By the time they arrived at the subway station, he was too concerned with thoughts of Sam's safety to be angry with her anymore, especially since his anger had actually been jealousy. "Sam, this place is a zoo. I'm not sure we should do this." It was noon, and there were people everywhere. Josh felt confused and overwhelmed by the pulsing crowd as well as the loud hissing and jangling sounds in the subway station.

"Josh, it's going to be okay. I promise you'll have fun. Come on." Taking his hand, she tugged him through the turnstile and onto the subway just before the pneumatic doors closed. It was too crowded to sit, so they simply stood together. Josh reached for one of the overhead grips in order to keep his balance, but Sam was too short unless she stood on her toes. Seeing her dilemma, Josh put his arm around her waist to keep her steady.

The farther south they rode, the more the train began to empty until at last there were several seats available, but Sam and Josh made no move to sit down. Neither of them realized they were still standing close together with his hand on her waist and her hand on his chest until they reached their stop. Then they quickly broke apart and exited the train without touching.

Sam pulled out a map and began to study it.

"Did Ethan the Perfect give you that?" he asked.

"Yes," she said evenly, unaffected by his sullen tone. "We're here, and we want to go here, so we need to go two blocks that way and four blocks that way." She stuffed the map in her bag and they set off.

They made their way to Bowling Green Park near Wall Street. The bull wasn't difficult to find because he was the main attraction in the park. For a few minutes, they stood back admiring him, and then Sam took the ubiquitous photo of Josh pretending to wrangle the bull. Of course he wanted to simply stand next to it, but she cajoled him into putting on the little charade, much to his chagrin.

"I can't believe you got me to do that," he said.

"I think there's a secret part of you that wanted to," she said. "Why else would you have capitulated?"

Because you're pretty, and I wanted to make you smile, he thought. That little voice that admitted to having feelings for her was really beginning to get on his nerves. He missed the angry voice that accused her of doing all manner of evil things.

After visiting the bull, they grabbed a hot dog from a street vendor and ate while they walked. Their next step was the site of the former World Trade Centers. They stood in sad, awed silence as they thought about that day and what had occurred. The people around them must have felt the same way because there was a sort of eerie silence all around the memorial site, as if no one wanted to speak out loud.

They stayed for a few minutes, paying proper respect to the memorial, and then hopped another subway to head to Rockefeller Center.

"That's where they put the tree," Sam said, pointing. "And that's where people skate." It was late summer, so there was no Christmas tree or ice skaters. Josh noticed her wistful tone.

"You'd like to see it at Christmas, huh?" he asked.

"Yes," she admitted. "I've seen it in so many movies. I guess it's sort of one of those romantic dreams girls have, to come here and skate and admire the tree."

"Maybe we could come back in the winter," Josh said, and couldn't believe his own ears. What was he doing? Wasn't he supposed to hope that she was out of the house by December? And, even if she wasn't, why would he be the one to accompany her on her return trip? Then again, if he didn't come along she might be left to the mercy of that Ethan guy. He could just picture the two of them skating together, holding hands. What if that other man kissed her?

"Why do you look so angry?" she asked, taking note of his fists which were now clenched tightly at his sides.

"No reason," he said. "Are you hungry?"

"What do you think?" she asked.

"I think I'm hungry even if you're not. Did the almighty Ethan suggest a dinner place for us?"

"He made some suggestions, but I thought we could wander around until we find something that looks good."

Eventually they decided on a burger joint. Sam was concerned Josh would balk at the high prices the hip-looking restaurant charged, but he didn't. In fact, he admitted to enjoying the food so much he polished off anything Sam couldn't eat, which was a lot because the portions were large.

"If I keep eating everything you don't, I'm going to get fat," Josh said.

"Better you than me," Sam said.

Josh froze. "Is that why you don't eat? Are you worried about getting fat?" A feeling of dread settled in the pit of his stomach. Did she have anorexia?

"Of course not," she said. "I'm honestly not hungry very often, and I can't eat when I get stressed; it makes me sick." He still didn't look convinced. She reached across the table and clasped his hand. "Honest, Josh, I'm not sick, and I'm not purposely starving myself. I eat when I'm hungry or when I remember. Plus, I don't burn that many calories sitting behind a desk all day. I ate a lot more when I was doing ranch work."

The reminder of her previous job working with him brought a rush of familiar anger to him and he snatched his hand from hers. "Ready?" he asked.

She rose and followed him from the restaurant with a sigh. It had been a lovely day together; why did she have to ruin it by mentioning their past? Now they would undoubtedly return to Belle and Cam's tiny apartment and try to avoid each other all night in the cramped space.

"Which way?" Josh asked.

"That way." She pointed toward the direction of the apartment.

"But that way is back home," he said. Noting her confused expression, he continued. "I meant which way to the park? You still want to see Central Park, don't you?"

"I do," she said, sounding not at all certain. "Do you?"

"I do," he answered, some anger still simmering in his tone. "A promise is a promise," he explained. "I don't go back on my word."

Meaning she did, apparently. Although she wasn't sure what word she had ever gone back on. "I don't want you to do this if this is how it's going to be," she said.

"What are you talking about?" he asked.

"This," she indicated him with a flourish of her hand. "I don't want to go to the park with you if you're going to be sullen and grumpy the whole time. It's supposed to be fun, not retribution or a promise kept by a twist of your arm."

"So I'll make it fun," he snapped.

"You're off to a great start," she responded irritably.

They entered the park in angry silence, but the beauty and serenity had a softening effect on both of them.

"There," Josh said a few minutes later. "Fun." He pointed to a carousel. They waited in line and took their turn riding in a circle. When they happened to glance at each other, they shared a smile.

When they finished the ride, Josh tugged her sleeve. "Come on, I got a line on some more fun." He began to jog, and she ran along behind him, trying not to giggle. After the carousel and now their unbidden sprint through the park, she felt like a little kid again. Josh stopped short at the edge of a lake and they stood in another line until Sam realized they were waiting for their turn to rent a rowboat.

The sun was beginning to dip when they reached the front of the line.

"Sorry," the ticketing agent said. "We close at dusk."

Josh leaned in and said something to the guy who miraculously relented and rented them a boat.

"What did you say to him?" she asked.

"I said I was from Montana and had promised you some fun," he said. Actually, he had said a whole lot more than that, such as how he was trying to impress a pretty girl who was angry with him. But there was no need to tell her all that. He helped her into the boat and rowed them to the middle of the lake.

"It's so beautiful here," she said.

Josh nodded. "I didn't expect this. I thought it would be all buildings, people, and pollution. But this is awesome." The sun began glinting on the lake as it made its descent for the day. The sky was streaked with red and purple. Most likely the haze was caused by pollution, but Josh didn't care; it was beautiful.

"I love it," she said. "I've loved today. It's spectacular."

Josh frowned. "Would you move here?"

She was surprised by the question. Didn't he know how much she loved Montana and country life? Didn't he understand that the reason she had loved the day so much was because of him? The city was awe-inspiring and lovely, but without him it would have been ho-hum and a little bit scary. But how to tell him without giving too much of herself away?

"I don't think I would move here," she said. "I'm a small-town girl at heart."

"But you've done so well here today," Josh said. Without her, he would have remained at Cam and Belle's apartment, staring out the window and wondering why anyone in his right mind would live here.

"Because I felt safe with you," she admitted. "If I were on my own, I wouldn't have been brave enough to explore." To avoid his gaze, she watched her finger as it trailed in the water at the side of the boat.

"I wouldn't have left the apartment without you," he admitted. Actually, without her, he would never have come to New York in the first place.

"We make a good team," she said. *Still.* Two years ago, they had worked seamlessly together, each picking up the slack for the other and doing what needed to be done without asking.

Now it was Josh's turn to stare at the water. Sam was beginning to settle into the corner of his heart she had left vacant two years ago, and he wasn't at all sure he liked that. What if she left again? How would he ever heal that hollow space? She had been his best friend; she had understood him like no one else in his life. Losing her had felt like a death. What if he lost her again? What if he found out some other horrible secret that separated them forever?

"We should get back," he said. He began rowing them toward the shore.

"Want me to row for a while?"

He laughed. "What do you think?"

"I think you've forgotten I'm a lot stronger than I look," she said.

"Have at it," he said, extending the oars to her. She settled them into place and began to row. The physical exertion felt good. She hadn't given her muscles a good workout since she left the ranch. Then she had been in the best shape of her life from riding her horse all day, fixing fences, and pulling calves. It had been nice not to have people defer to her because of her sex. The expectation that she could pull her weight had possibly been the one thing she enjoyed about her charade.

For the last two years since the accident, everyone had treated her like a fragile China doll. It was difficult to be angry about it when people meant well, but she longed for the chance to do work that required more than her brain.

Josh sat back and stretched out his legs, his hands laced behind his head. Seeing the determined look on Sam's face as she painstakingly rowed them toward the shore reminded him of all the times he had watched her working on the ranch. Of course at the time he had thought he was watching a small man, and he had been amused by the extra effort it took him to do what came so easily to everyone else. But Sam hadn't complained. Ever.

He tried to picture Chelsea working on the ranch and almost laughed. Chelsea was the type of girl who would wear black mourning clothes if she broke a nail. He had always thought he preferred his women to be feminine and girly, but he was rethinking that. As he watched Sam struggle with the heavy oars, there was nothing manly about her. She was small and delicate, but determined.

It was the determination he admired, he realized. No matter what life threw at her, she was determined to see it through. In retrospect, he was appalled by some of the difficult, exhausting work she had had to perform on the ranch. If he had known it was a woman he was working with, he never would have assigned her to tasks like dispatching injured calves or killing errant rattlesnakes. But Sam had faced every task with grit, and she had seen every task through to careful completion. When he pictured her as she had been with her choppy short hair and ill-fitting Stetson, he saw her for the first time as a woman. Oddly, she hadn't lost her womanliness because she did a man's work.

The sun was just ending its journey when Josh helped Sam from the boat. They walked in silence for a while until Josh tugged her sleeve again.

"One more thing," he said.

Once again they stood in line until it was their turn to rent one of the cozy-looking carriages. The dapple-gray horse stood patiently while Josh helped Sam into the carriage. Thankfully their driver was the silent type who let them enjoy the beauty of the scenery without comment. Sam slipped her arm into the crook of Josh's elbow and rested her hand on his bicep.

"This is the perfect ending to a perfect day, Josh. Thank you." She smiled up at him. The first hints of moonlight glinted off her pale skin, making her look even more fragile than she actually was. He wanted to kiss her, but he was all too aware of their driver sitting two feet away, as well as the crowds of people still milling the park. Instead he settled for simply looking at her while she looked at him. They were missing the scenery of the park, but they were taking each other in, seeing new things they had never noticed, and revealing more with their eyes than they would ever say with their lips.

All too soon, the ride was over. Josh lifted her down and reluctantly released her when her feet hit the ground. They walked in silence back to the apartment. The walk was long and should have required a cab, but neither of them was in a hurry because both wanted time to clear their heads.

But when they arrived at the apartment, neither of their heads was clear. Sam put her hand on the doorknob, but Josh held her back.

"Sam, I…" That was as far as he got because he had no idea what to say to her. *I can't forgive you, but I can't stop my attraction to you,* or *I can't stop thinking about you, but I don't think I'll ever stop being angry at you?* Neither of those things was appropriate to say. Instead, he blurted the next best thing that came to mind. "I broke up with Chelsea."

For Sam who knew Chelsea had always been Josh's dream, the news came as a bombshell. "Josh, why?"

His fingers brushed her waist. "You know why."

"I'm sorry," she said, unbidden tears clogging her throat. "I never meant to cause you trouble. Again."

Slowly, gently, he slipped his arms around her and drew her against him. She rested her head on his chest, wrapped her arms around him, and they clung to each other in silence a few minutes before opening the door and stepping inside.

CHAPTER 17

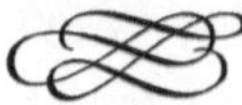

Somehow Sam slept. After her strange encounter in the hallway with Josh and the lingering tension between them, she thought she would lie awake all night. But almost as soon as her head hit the pillow, she was out.

Similarly, Josh slept. He woke first and lay watching Sam above him on the couch. She was so close, and yet so far, which was becoming the story of their lives. They lived in the same house, but there was still an emotional gulf between them he didn't ever see going away. He was honest enough to admit he was horribly attracted to her, both physically and as a person, but he also knew he could never really have her. There was too much unknown about her, she wasn't the right girl for him, and she had hurt him once before. But when she opened her eyes and looked down at him, that information did nothing to stop him from reaching up to take her hand, smiling like the Sam addict he was becoming.

"Hey," he whispered. His free hand reached up and brushed the hair at her temple, so dark and thick and pretty. She blinked at him, blue eyes big and deep.

"Hey," she said groggily, smiling tentatively in return. "Ready to go home?"

"Not as much as I thought I would be. I had fun," he said.

"So did I. But I'm ready to go home. I miss Nikita and the puppies and Ivy's stallion."

"Probably not as much as they miss you." He laid her hand on his chest and pressed his hand on top of it, inadvertently placing it over his heart. They lay that way, looking at each other, until the knob turned on Cam and Belle's door. Then Josh rolled away and stood up, leaving Sam's hand to drop uselessly to the floor. She didn't disagree they should keep whatever was broiling between them away from his family, but the fact that he was so eager to do so still stung.

It was Saturday, so Belle had more leeway with her schedule. The four of them shared a leisurely breakfast together at another restaurant before a car came to take Sam and Josh to the airport. Cam and Belle would be staying for another month before they returned to Montana again.

There were hugs all around. Sam was surprised when she was included in the emotional display. After a few final goodbyes, Cam and Belle stood arm in arm waving from the curb while Josh and Sam drove away, their faces turned to peer through the back of the cab. Although the car wasn't a limousine, there was a glass divider between them and the driver, so it felt private in the backseat. They faced forward, a silence somewhere between awkward and comfortable hovering between them. Josh wasn't certain if the awkwardness was from his new awareness of her or his old resentment of her.

Sam was wearing one of her new pretty skirts. Josh took advantage of the opportunity to rest his hand on her bare knee, his thumb making slow circles around her kneecap. Other than that small touch, they didn't communicate until they were on the plane, and then they sat talking and not touching for the entire flight. After they reviewed the highlights of their trip together, they plotted ways to try and keep all six of Nikita's puppies.

"You could give one to Tanner for a wedding present," Sam suggested. "That's almost like keeping it in the family."

"I could give one to you," Josh said, tipping his head to bestow a smile. He was flirting with her, but he couldn't seem to help it.

"Oh." Sam's face fell.

"What? I thought that would make you happy."

"It would except I would have to leave it when I go away. I would never be able to find an appropriate place to live with that kind of dog."

Josh scowled at her, his stomach dropping. "Are you already plotting your next escape?"

"I'm being realistic, Josh. This situation isn't forever. You've made it clear you don't want me here, so I don't understand why you're angry with me for trying to plan for my future. What am I supposed to do, stay at the ranch forever as Belle's secretary? Stand by and watch while you get married and move your wife into the room across from mine?"

"How long are you planning to stay?" he asked.

"Until the situation becomes unbearable," she said truthfully.

"It's already unbearable," he mumbled. The confusion was making him irritable, and the attraction he couldn't quell was making him crazy, like an itch he couldn't reach. But he didn't want her to leave; he wasn't ready for that, not even close.

Sam, however, misunderstood his meaning. How could he say such a thing after a perfect two days together? "I'm sorry you feel that way," she whispered, turning her head to the side to hide her silent tears.

For the rest of the ride they remained quiet, each lost in thought and boiling emotion.

The next morning, the silence remained during breakfast. But it was Sunday, and Sunday meant church.

"Are you coming?" Josh asked, still grumpy.

"Am I allowed?" Sam replied, equally terse.

"Don't be crazy," Josh said. "It's church. Everyone is allowed."

"I'll go," she said, scurrying to her room to change into a dress. They met in the kitchen and took a moment to admire each other. Josh always wore a suit to church, and Sam loved that about him. Sometimes his old-fashioned ideals were maddening, but other times, like now, they were charming.

"You look very pretty."

His tone was so begrudging she laughed. "Thank you, and you look very dashing."

"Dashing?" he repeated. Her tone was much sunnier than his had been, and he couldn't stop his smile. "Who says that anymore?" Nonetheless, his cheeks were slightly pink from the compliment. He helped her into the truck, for which she was thankful. It wasn't easy to hoist oneself into a tall truck while wearing a dress.

They remained quiet on the ride to church, but the silence no longer felt angry. Instead, Sam was nervous. She hadn't attended church much in her life. Occasionally someone would get the idea to host a worship service on the rodeo circuit—some of their cowboys were more religious than others. Sam always attended, and she always enjoyed the singing and the words. God fascinated her, even though she didn't know much about Him. Church, however, was unsettling. Everyone looked fresh, pretty, and blameless, as if they had never had a problem in their lives. They knew all the songs and when to sit and when to stand. Sam knew none of those things.

Josh, who wasn't known for his perception into the female psyche, for once guessed at what was making her so jittery. "Relax," he leaned down to whisper as they took their place in his normal pew. "I'll show you what to do. Everyone is friendly here."

She nodded and looked up at him with such a look of trusting adoration the gossip mill went into immediate overdrive. *Josh and Sam? What happened to Josh and Chelsea? Of course it was bound to happen with her living in his house. Maybe they had been together all along like people suspected. How else did he explain the fact that he worked so closely with her and never knew she was a woman?*

For the moment, though, the couple in question was oblivious to the thoughts circulating about them. They sat a discreet distance apart and didn't touch or talk during the sermon. To their naïve way of thinking, that would dispel any hints of romance between them.

Neither of them noticed the lone figure in the back of the room who never took her eyes off them.

Chelsea had also never been to this church. She told Josh it was because she preferred her family's Lutheran church down the street, but she never attended there, either. Most Sundays she preferred sleeping in. Occasionally she was working off a hangover. Whatever the reason, she had no plans to spend her day off dressing up and listening to a boring sermon.

But then Josh broke up with her. In addition to the humiliation of the event, there was the seething anger. She had never been angrier at anyone in her life than she was at Joshua King, unless it was that stupid cow beside him, Sam McCoy. If Chelsea didn't need his money and security so badly, she would gladly write him off because she was pretty sure she actually hated him. No one, however, was allowed to dump her, and especially not for the likes of a bug-eyed, oddball little orphan. So, stuffing down her rage, she woke early and dressed for church.

For the past few days she had half expected Josh to come crawling back to her, admitting he had made a terrible mistake. Everyone knew he'd had a huge crush on her for most of their lives. What had once been flattering had quickly turned to loathing when they started dating—he was so *boring*. But she liked knowing the power she held over him. The fact that one of the high and might Kings wanted her had given her an exalted position in the town she hadn't previously known was possible. But Josh hadn't come crawling back, and the thought that he might instead be running toward another woman was enough to push Chelsea over the edge. She found herself doing whatever it took to win him back, even if it involved church. She would play the sweet innocent until they were married, and then she would spend the rest of her life making him pay for the sin of humiliating her in front of this town.

Now she sat at the back of the church, ignoring the music and preaching, and focusing instead on the couple near up front, sitting possessively in the Kings' pew. They weren't touching or talking, but there was still something between them. Chelsea, an astute observer of other women for the sake of competition, could feel it. Maybe it was the way he held the hymnal for her, or the way he pointed to the correct passage in his Bible. Maybe it was the way she looked at him with her giant cow eyes, as if he were her every dream come true. If she weren't so angry, Chelsea would have been amused by that. *He's not as great as he seems, unless you enjoy watching paint dry,* she wanted to say. The dullest, most aggravating hours of her life had been spent with Joshua King. If not for his family's wealth and the fact that he was an excellent kisser, she might not have been able to stand it as long as she had.

After church was finished, she stood in the back waiting for Josh to notice her. When he failed to do so, her immeasurable rage increased another notch. "Hey, Josh," she said softly, stepping forward into his line of vision. Her eyes filled with tears she didn't have to force; all she had to do was think of the King's money going to waste on some other girl and she wanted to cry.

Sam, the little twit, flinched and backed toward the door. "I'll wait at the truck," she announced. What did she think was going to happen? Did she think Chelsea was going to have a throw-down in the middle of church? Chelsea smiled, enjoying the thought. It would feel good to beat the other girl's face in, and she might do it, too, if she thought she could get away with it.

"Hi, Chelsea," Josh said, his tone laced with sympathy and something like guilt. That was good; she could work with guilt. "How are you?"

"The truth? I'm worried about you."

He frowned. "Me? Why?"

She took a breath and held it, pressing her lips together as if she didn't want to say. Thinking of the King's money had given her an idea. "You know I don't like talking badly about other people, but… No, never mind. Forget I said anything." She tried to slip past him, but of course he held her back, the stupid, predictable imbecile.

"Chelsea, what's wrong? Are you in some kind of trouble? Do you need something?"

Hmm, feigning an emergency would be a good tactic for another time, but not right now. Right now she had to plant the seed of sedition. "No, I'm not in trouble. You are." She clamped her lips together again. "I shouldn't have said that."

Josh's frown deepened. "Chelsea, what is it?"

She could tell her moment had come because he was beginning to lose patience. "I heard something in town the other day, and I wanted to warn you, but I don't know how to say it without looking like a jealous idiot, which I am," she added with a pathetic swipe at her brimming eyes. "But I care about you too much to see you laughed at again."

Josh's ears perked up. "Laughed at? What are you talking about?"

"Well, you know Tanner's girl, Lizzie, at the diner?"

"No, not personally," he said. He had only heard about her from Sam.

The fact that he didn't know her was good; that would certainly help Chelsea's story. "We've sort of become friends, and she was laughing the other day. At you. She didn't know about us, and she was telling me about this whole plot that Sam has hatched to get you interested in her. She said now that she's living at your ranch and you're the only single brother, she figures she'll trap you into marriage and have all your money at her disposal."

Now it was Josh's turn to seethe. "That's a lie," he said. "Sam would never do that. She doesn't care about money."

"Doesn't she?" Chelsea asked. "All girls care about money and security Josh. We like to be taken care of." *Hint, hint.*

"I don't believe that," Josh said, but he sounded less certain.

"I knew you wouldn't," Chelsea said sadly. "You're too good to believe anyone is bad." That part was true. He had certainly glossed over any rumors about her. "Maybe it's not true; maybe Lizzie made the whole thing up, although I don't know why she would." She shrugged. "I've done my part, and you've been duly warned." She turned to go and paused without looking back at him. "I miss you," she whispered, then rushed out of the church before the words could trigger her gag reflex.

Josh strode to the truck and slammed the door. Sam studied him, trying to judge how upset he was. Very, she thought, which was why she was surprised when he spoke.

"Let's eat at the diner today," he said.

"Okay," she drawled. The diner would put them on display for the entire town, something she assumed he would avoid at all costs.

"Will Tanner's girl be working?" he asked.

"I have no idea," she said, still wondering what his problem was. What could Chelsea possibly have said that would make him have the sudden and pressing need to meet Lizzie? Knowing what a schemer Chelsea was, it could be anything. A part of her wanted to ask, but she knew Josh probably didn't trust her enough to tell her. That hurt more than anything Chelsea might have said.

It took less than a minute to drive to the diner. Josh was so intent on his purpose he failed to open Sam's door or help her down from the too-tall truck. She shimmied out, trying not to flash the world at large when her dress rode high on her thighs.

Because it was Sunday, and because half the town had been released from church, they had to wait to be seated at the diner. Lizzie was working. She smiled and waved at Sam before returning to work.

"That her?" Josh asked.

"Yes, that's her," Sam said, frowning up at Josh. She knew his look, knew how hard-edged he could be when he was upset. For whatever reason that look was now aimed at Lizzie. "You're going to be nice to her, aren't you? She's sweet, and you wouldn't want to do anything to alienate Tanner."

She had a point. Begrudgingly, he decided to withhold judgment until he met the woman. She had a nice smile and didn't look like the type to indulge in malicious gossip, but who could tell? Sam didn't look capable of pulling off a long-lasting deception, but she had.

Finally it was their turn to be seated. They weren't in Lizzie's section, but she came over to say hello.

"Lizzie, this is Josh," Sam introduced.

"Oh, *Josh*," Lizzie said significantly. "I've heard a lot about you. It's nice to meet you." She flashed him another quick smile before scurrying off to refill one of her customer's drinks.

"Why has she heard a lot about me?" Josh asked Sam, his tone suspicious.

Sam's cheeks pinked. She glanced down, fiddling with her silverware. She hadn't realized she had talked so much about Josh, but apparently she had. "I, um, may have mentioned you a time or two."

"What did you say?" He forced his voice to a harsh whisper in order to avoid yelling. He couldn't believe Chelsea had been correct and Sam had been talking about him.

Reluctantly Sam's gaze met his, her cheeks flushing a deeper shade of crimson. "I told her about how you had the idea to use the dogs to help with the work. Tanner agreed they helped make life simpler. Then we talked about Nikita and the puppies. I invited her to the ranch to see them. I hope that was okay."

That softened him slightly. "Was that it?"

"I, um, may have mentioned you're good with the animals and that you prefer working with the animals to working in the office." Embarrassingly, she also remembered that she had expounded on Josh's skill, bravery, and strength for a long time. And she may have stated that she thought him the nicest looking of all the brothers. There was no way she was telling him that, though. "What exactly did Chelsea say to you?"

"She…nothing." Sam wasn't lying, that much he knew. And Chelsea hadn't lied, so that meant this Lizzie must have made everything up for some reason. He had hoped to like the woman Tanner was going to marry, but that wasn't going to happen. At least he wouldn't have to have a lot of contact with her, and he didn't want Sam to, either.

"I don't want you to spend any more time with Lizzie," he said.

"What?" Sam asked. "Why not? She's the sweetest person I've met in ages. She's funny, thoughtful, and a hard worker. She's been putting in tons of extra hours to try and save up for a house for herself and Tanner."

That didn't sound like someone who spent her spare time spreading malicious gossip, but to be on the safe side, Josh wanted to keep his distance for a while. But saying so to Sam might cause her to dig her heels in and defy him; she could be obstinate that way sometimes. Strangely, she seemed to follow everyone else's commands without question.

"Why don't you ever do what I tell you to do?" he asked, exasperated.

"Because I know you too well to think your motives are pure, and I trust you enough to tell you no."

That was a maddening answer. She wasn't supposed to continue to know him so well, and she wasn't supposed to trust him so much. In fact, she should be little more than a stranger to him. She should be his family's employee and nothing more. Maybe then he and Chelsea wouldn't have broken up. Maybe Lizzie wasn't the only one he needed to keep his distance from. Maybe taking a break from Sam would help him figure out the confusing muddle his thoughts and emotions had become.

Sam sensed his emotional withdrawal like a physical thing. He still sat in the same position, but it was as if he had closed himself up and moved away. Although she didn't know its cause, she was almost certain it had something to do with Chelsea.

Please don't let him end up with her. She could stand Josh's continued anger and unforgiveness, but she absolutely would not, could not see him tied to someone so far beneath him. Even if Josh never forgave Sam completely and let her into his heart again, she hoped he wouldn't fall for Chelsea again. He could do much better. She wanted to tell him, but knew he wouldn't listen. Not only was Josh the type of person who had to learn hard truths for himself, he wouldn't appreciate her unrequited input on his life, especially not with the breakup looming over them as it did now.

They finished their lunch in silence, drove home quietly, and retreated to their rooms for the rest of the day, each wary and suspicious of the other.

CHAPTER 18

Their silent standoff continued for the next few days. They ate breakfast and supper together, spoke polite phrases to each other such as, "Pass the butter, please," but otherwise didn't talk.

After supper Josh went to his room to do whatever he did in there —sulk, perhaps?—and Sam went to hers to read a book. She had decided to be patient and wait him out. The peace between them lately had been too good to be true. She knew Josh well enough to realize he was still working through his issues where she was concerned. One step forward, two steps back. She was convinced if she left him alone, he would come around and eventually learn to forgive her. At least, that was her hope.

In reality she was finding it difficult not to be hurt and discouraged by his shunning. As the week wore on and there was no change in him, she began having trouble sleeping. She was lonely and sad. Thoughts of her life kept her up as she tried to figure out where she had gone wrong and what she could do differently. How long was she going to stay here waiting for any scrap of affection from Josh? Wasn't it sort of degrading to be at his mercy all the time? But every time she decided the answer was yes, she realized she had nowhere else to go. Excluding the crisis it caused in her personal life, this job was amazing. She was finally making enough to live on, as well as adding a substantial amount to her meager savings every week. Even if she only stuck it out a few months, she would have some security when she moved on and she wouldn't have to sink as low as she had when she had lived behind the feed mill.

All these thoughts were swirling in her mind late Friday night when a strange sound from outside caused her to sit up in alarm. Was that Nikita barking? Since her puppies had been born, Nikita had stayed close to the barn, not leaving their sides, especially at night. What could draw her out and cause her to bark at two in the morning?

Sam's room was on the barn side of the house, so she knew Josh couldn't have heard what she did. She strained her ears, listening harder, and, though she couldn't identify what they were, she heard other strange sounds, too. Something was going on. Throwing off her covers, she darted across the hall and banged on Josh's door. He answered it with his hair disheveled, gun in hand.

"What is it?" he asked, still half asleep.

"I think someone's outside. I heard Nikita barking."

"Stay here," he said, shoving past her. He was barefoot, she noted. She darted into his room, grabbed his shoes, and followed him onto the porch. By the time she reached the porch, it was all over. Josh had already fired a warning shot into the air, and the strange truck and trailer were speeding down the long lane and out of sight.

Sam followed him from the porch, realizing as she did so she was also barefoot. The lights at Coy and Cade's houses flared to life. Their houses were farther away from the main barn, but not so far away that they would have missed the loud gunshot.

"Did they get him?" Sam asked, straining her eyes to see if Ivy's stallion was still in his corral. Since the truck had been parked right in front of his enclosure, he was the obvious target. With relief, she heard his frightened whinny. "Thank goodness," she said, pressing her hand to her heart. "It's okay, boy," she soothed. Standing on her toes, she reached up to pat him, but before she could reach him, she heard a strangled cry from Josh.

Looking down, she bit back a cry of her own. Nikita lay between them in a pool of blood so large there was no way she could still be alive.

"Oh," Sam said. She reached out her hand, either toward Nikita's lifeless form or Josh's prone figure bent over her, she wasn't sure. But when his head whipped up, she froze at the sight of the raw anger in his expression.

"Why didn't you wake me sooner? I could have saved her." He bent his head once again and picked Nikita up, cradling her lifeless form to his chest.

"What is it? What happened?" Coy ran up behind her, but Sam couldn't say a word. She dropped Josh's shoes in front of him, turned, and sprinted to the house.

Despite her frenzied flight through the kitchen and down the hall to her room, she was calm when she took out all of her new suitcases and began packing her clothes. She had had it; implicating her in Nikita's death had been the final straw. How he could be so irrational, cold, and mean was beyond her. From this point on she was washing her hands of Joshua King. He could enjoy his ivory tower until he either died alone or found some other patsy to waste away, eating her heart out over him. Though she would be willing to bet there were few women with the emotional stamina to take him on. He was like hugging barbed wire most of the time, only less warm and more hurtful.

"What are you doing?"

She had almost finished packing when he stood in the doorway of her room and spoke.

"What does it look like?" she asked wearily. "I'm leaving. You win, Josh. I can't take it anymore. You hate me, and you don't want me here. I get it."

"How could you think I meant what I said?" he asked. "I know it wasn't your fault."

"I don't care what you meant. I'm tired of being your punching bag."

He winced. "Then don't be. Stand up to me; you're the only one who can. Don't let me get away with stuff like that."

She whirled on him and threw the hanger in her hand, striking the wall opposite. "Do you think I felt like arguing with you when I saw her lying there? I loved that dog." Her voice broke. He went forward and swept her into his arms. She was too tired to resist. Instead, she cried on his chest, great heaving sobs. Only when her tears started to die down did she realize he was crying, too. He had loved Nikita even more than she had, and for much longer.

"I'm sorry," he said. "I'm sorry I said something so horrible. I shouldn't have. You know my first reaction to anything is always anger. I didn't mean it, of course I didn't. I know it wasn't your fault."

"I can't take it anymore, Josh. You're hurting me. I think it would be best if I left so we can both get out of this unhealthy situation." Despite her words, she clung. At the moment she felt like his solid form was the only thing keeping her upright. Not only was she in pain over Nikita, she was so weary, so very tired of fighting all her battles on her own. She desperately wanted to lean on someone and, out of everyone she'd ever known, Josh seemed the only one fit for the job.

"Don't go, Sam," he said brokenly, clinging to her as desperately as she clung to him. If someone walked in on them in that moment, it would be difficult to tell where one of their bodies ended and the other began. "Please don't go, Sam, *please.*" He shuddered, or maybe she did. Pressed tightly together as they were, they shuddered together. His hand eased to the small of her back and flattened, attempted to pull her impossibly closer.

A whimper from the hallway drew her attention. "What's that?" she asked, reluctantly peeling her head from his thumping heart.

"It's the puppies. They're still a good two weeks from being weaned. I need your help with them. Please? They need you; I need you. We all need you." His hands cupped her face, pressing over her ears, staring plaintively into her eyes. He was beautiful, even more than usual with a soft, contrite expression on his face for once. His eyes were red-rimmed and teary and it took everything within her not to stand on her toes and kissed them closed. Her hands smoothed over his bare chest until they made purchase with his shoulders, gripping them to keep herself in check.

"Are you really using puppies to emotionally blackmail me into staying?" she asked. Her voice was raw and broken.

"I am," he said. His voice was the same.

"You're pathetic," she said.

"Admittedly. Does that mean you'll stay?" he asked.

"You know I will," she answered wearily. It might kill her, might shatter her heart into a million pieces, but she couldn't go as long as he asked her to stay. He let her go, eyes darting fleetingly up and down her pajama-clad body before he stepped away. She stood back while he dragged the box of puppies into her bathroom. They closed the door and sat on the floor, watching the puppies explore their new surroundings, trying to come to terms with their shock, their grief, their raw and spent emotions.

"What happened?" she asked at last.

"Rustlers, trying to steal Ivy's horse, like we thought. Coy called the sheriff, but I doubt they left any evidence behind. They bashed Nikita in the head with something as soon as she barked."

"Do you think they'll try again?" she asked.

"There's no doubt in my mind," he said.

She shuddered. He put his arm around her, pulling her close against his side, his thumb gliding lazily along the length of her neck. Her arm eased over his stomach, clinging. He kissed the top of her head. They leaned against the wall and watched the puppies for a long time until she finally fell asleep, then he carried her to bed. He paused a moment to watch her sleep, thinking how peaceful she looked, how right, how perfect. At last when the temptation to stay became too great, he took a breath and eased from her room.

* * *

AFTER THAT, they shared a common purpose: keep the puppies alive. Although they were much less frail than when they were newborns, they still required around the clock care, feedings every few hours, and cleaning with a warm washcloth to encourage them to use the bathroom. They also wanted to play at all hours. Sam and Josh took turns getting up with them in the night, but they were still both exhausted.

"This must be what it's like to have a baby," Josh said groggily as he stared into his coffee mug one morning, a few days in.

Sam grunted a reply.

Josh smiled at her. "I thought you were a morning person. What happened to my Little Mary Sunshine?"

"She inherited six puppies who don't believe in sleep."

"Two weeks seems like a long time, but it will go by quickly," Josh assured her.

"But even after they're weaned, we can't turn them loose. They'll need to stay in my bathroom for another month at least."

"You could move into my room" Josh said. When his suggestion was met with silence, he hastened to add, "And I would move into your room. We could switch rooms so I could be closer to the puppies. That was what I meant. Not, uh, the other thing."

She smiled at his sheepish expression. "Thanks, but I'll make it; it'll be okay. And they are adorable. Does the sheriff have any leads on the thieves?"

Josh shook his head. "No. There was no evidence. We're thinking of installing video surveillance so at least if something happens we can get them on tape, maybe get a license plate. Otherwise, we've done everything we can to protect ourselves."

"I feel like we're sitting ducks," she said. "How's Ivy doing?"

"She's blaming herself for bringing the horse here and making us a target. Never mind how much income she's already added to the ranch, it's not her fault someone wants to steal from us. If it wasn't the horse, it would be something else. Thieves are thieves; stealing hard-earned possessions from other people is what they do."

"It takes a whole lot of entitlement to think you deserve what someone else has," she said angrily.

He grinned at her, thinking sleep-tousled and riled was a potent combination. "Preach it, sister." He drained his coffee and carried his mug to the sink. "I should go. I'll stop in later and take my turn feeding the dogs." He bent and kissed her forehead and froze. The action had been instinctive. If he had been thinking rationally, he certainly wouldn't have done it. But now that he had, he wanted to do it again, and on the lips this time.

They remained frozen, staring at each other. "I should go, too" she whispered at last, breaking the spell between them. He backed up a step before turning to charge from the house.

Sam waited until she heard the front door close, and then she slumped in her chair, resting her head in her hands. She had come so close to giving in and allowing Josh to kiss her. It was what she wanted, but she couldn't do it, not until the issues between them were completely resolved. If she allowed him to act on the attraction between them, they might never heal their friendship. Right now, they were edging toward reconciliation and she couldn't do anything that might damage that, even if it meant refraining from the most temptation she had ever faced. Josh wanted her, she was aware enough to realize. But she wanted more than his helpless attraction; she wanted his heart.

Before her mind could torture her with thoughts of what it would be like to kiss Josh, she poured another cup of coffee and took it to her office to start her day.

ive days later, they were still exhausted and still on pins and needles, waiting for the other shoe to drop, waiting for the thieves to make their next move. Between the anxiety and the sleeplessness with the puppies, Sam and Josh were on edge and irritable. But for once they weren't taking their moods out on each other. Instead, they remained quiet, trying hard to tamp down their bad moods. After they finished supper every night, they retired to the den to watch a movie together.

Even though it was summer, the room was cool and they had developed the cozy ritual of sitting on the couch together under a blanket. Unknown to each other, they had each promised themselves it was too soon for a physical relationship. So they refrained from doing what they really wanted to do, which was reach for each other. Instead they sat side by side, snuggled under the blanket, and trying hard to concentrate on the movie despite the horrible and mounting tension humming between them.

On one such night Coy walked into the house in search of batteries for his flashlight. Muted voices from the den told him Sam and Josh were in that room. Being both curious and shameless, he crept to the den to see if he could catch them making out. But they were sitting silently side by side like two puritans with at least six inches between them beneath the cozy, easy-to-hide-under blanket he and Ivy had made so much use of in the early days of newlywed bliss.

"Hopeless," he mouthed. Rolling his eyes and shaking his head, he crept back down the hallway and out of the house.

* * *

ON FRIDAY afternoon the sound of a car alerted Sam to the fact that there was a visitor. Since visitors were few and far between, she was both curious and apprehensive as she stood and made her way down the hall to the porch. What if it was Chelsea come to call on Josh? Sam knew the other girl too well to think she had given up on him. It would be like her to drop in on a Friday night and demand his attention for the rest of the evening.

But when she opened the door and stepped onto the porch, she wished it was Chelsea who stood before her. In fact, she wished it was anyone else in the world but her horrible, terrifying stepfather.

"Sam-Sam," he said.

"Earl," Sam returned, trying to make her voice sound strong and not shaky like she felt. The sound of his voice, as well as the dreaded nickname, had haunted her teenage years. "What are you doing here?"

"Is that any way to greet your daddy?"

"You are not my father," she said vehemently, her anger flaring to uncontainable levels. The sight of him had the familiar effect of causing bile to rise in the back of her throat and she worked hard to push it back down.

His smug leer changed to a frown, strewn with hatred. "What do you think I'm doing here? I came to collect you. Get in the car." He pointed to the battered truck behind him.

"I'm not going anywhere with you." Automatically her hands slid behind her back, reaching for the safety of the house, for support. It was no good, though; she was too far away.

Earl took a step forward, but she held her ground. "Girl, I done spent the past four years looking for you. You belong to me. Now get in that car before I come up on that porch and make you."

This was her moment; this was what she had been working for, trying so hard to gain the confidence for. Her hands settled back at her sides, and she took a bold step forward. "I am not a girl. I am a twenty-year-old woman. And I do not belong to you. I never have. You were married to my mother, but you have no legal claim on me. Now get off this land before I have you thrown off."

He looked around, grinning. "I don't see no one who's going to make me leave." His gaze fastened greedily on her again, and she had to fight the urge to throw up. "You look real pretty and grown up in your fancy new clothes. But, see, I know what you been up to the last few years. I know you dressed like a boy. All I gotta do is find a friendly judge and tell him how you ran away from me and tried to pretend you was a boy. I'll tell them how your poor mother was worried sick about you and made me promise to care for her crazy daughter. I can get you declared incompetent and have you put in my charge. You know I can do it, too, I can see it in your eyes."

"No, you're lying. No judge in his right mind would give me to you. You're a dirty, filthy pervert, and I…" She didn't get any farther because he ran up the steps and hit her so hard across the face everything went black and she saw spots for a minute. He grabbed her upper arms and started to shake her roughly back and forth.

"You shut up and get in that car before I have to beat some more sense into you."

She opened her mouth to scream, but suddenly found she didn't need to. Earl released her. When her eyes opened, she realized why. He was now lying at the foot of the stairs and trying to scramble to a standing position. Josh stood in front of her, his hands on his hips, his gun resting on the porch behind him.

"Mister, you have two seconds to get off this land before I come down there and make you. If I ever see you hit her again, I'll put a bullet in you before either of us can blink."

Earl finally found his feet and stood swaying, trying to decide if he wanted to tangle with Josh. Josh must have hit him because his lip was split and his nose was trailing blood. Josh took a step down, and Earl turned, scrabbling for his truck in a panic. He started it and threw it into gear, leaving a trail of dust in his wake.

"Who was that man?" Josh asked slowly, eyes still on Earl's truck. The rage was so palpable in his body it left a metallic taste in his mouth. He had almost been hoping the man remained so he could hit him a few more times, might have the chance to beat him to a lifeless, bloody pulp. He hadn't seen him hit Sam, but he had seen him shaking her, and he could tell by the bloody streak under her nose and red welt on her cheek that she had been punched. If he had actually seen the man strike her, there was no telling what he might have done in response.

"That was my mother's husband," Sam said shakily. At last her need began to outweigh his vengeful rage. Slowly, Josh swiveled to look down at her, assessing. Her hair was a mess, her face battered and starting to swell. Something new gripped him from the inside, something he didn't recognize and couldn't name. She looked so scared and so…shattered.

"Come on," he said tenderly. Gently, he eased his arm around her and turned her in the direction of the house. He led her to his bathroom because the puppies would crawl all over them in hers. While that might work to distract and cheer her, he needed his sole focus on her for the time being.

"I need to get back to work," Sam said, trying to turn dazedly toward the office.

"You're taking the rest of the day off," Josh said in the new gentle tone. Pulling the cordless phone from the wall, he called Belle's private number. "It's Josh. Sam is sick and she's taking the rest of the day off. Thanks, I will. Bye." He hung up and stuffed the phone in his pocket, intending to return it to its cradle later. "Belle says to feel better."

Sam nodded as if the words meant anything, but all she could think was that her stepfather had found her and her life was over. For so many years now she had successfully evaded him, and he had found her here of all places, tainting the Kings with his evil merely by showing up. They couldn't be part of this, shouldn't have to know a person like him existed in the world. She was going to have to run. Again.

Ever so gently, Josh grasped her biceps and used them to set her on his closed toilet while he rifled through his medicine cabinet until he found what he wanted. He rinsed a cloth with cool water and gently swiped the blood from beneath her nose.

"Tell me about it," he urged softly.

She wrung her hands in her lap, staring at them with a mountain of shame, not wanting to talk about it. He used the cloth to tip her face up to his, his eyes penetrating all the way to her soul.

"Tell me, Samantha. All of it. Don't leave a word out."

For some reason, she complied. Maybe because she was so tired of dealing with it on her own. Maybe because, for once, Josh was looking at her like he used to, as if he cared, as if she were the most important person in the world to him. "When my mother was alive, he beat me sometimes. Nothing horrible, a smack here and there. Of course she knew about it, but she tried to pretend it wasn't happening. I was thirteen when she died. The beatings got worse, and then his interest in me changed. He started to watch me in a way that scared me, but I didn't know why. And then one night when I was fifteen, he…he came into my room. I ran away the next day, but he found me and dragged me back home, beating me until I passed out to make certain it wouldn't happen again.

"For a few months he left me alone, and then it happened again. I was sixteen then. I ran away again, but I had learned a few things by then. I disguised myself. No one was looking for a runaway boy, they're a dime a dozen. And I was afraid if other men like him found out I was a girl, they would do the same thing. So I cut off my hair and pretended to be a boy. I worked odd jobs, staying on the move until I wound up here when I was eighteen. I should have moved on. I knew he would find me eventually." She bit her lip and winced when she tasted the metallic sting of blood. She didn't remember him hitting her lip, but it must have been included in the blow to her cheek. "I'm going to have to move again." It was all she seemed to be able to focus on, her pressing need to get away, to protect herself, to protect the Kings' good name.

"No. You're staying right here," Josh said, his solemn tone leaving no room for disagreement. "Do you think I would let him get close to you again?" His hands shook with suppressed violence as he tried to dab gently at her wounds. Never had he felt such a potent combination of rage and tenderness. More than anything he wished he had known this information when he confronted the strange man; he would have dealt his own vengeance.

Sam was too far gone to hear the concern, only the anger. Her mind felt like it was spiraling toward panic, toward hysteria. "Didn't you hear what he said, Josh? He'll do it, too. Despite what you saw, he's charismatic. People like him; they believe him. Sometimes people questioned why I was always covered in bruises. He convinced them I was clumsy. If he says he'll find a judge who will grant him custody of me, he will. I don't know why he won't leave me alone, but it's like he's obsessed with me." She started to shake, pressing her hands to her temples to try and push back the mounting mania.

He knelt in front of her and rested his hands on her shoulders. "No, Sam, *no*. You're not being rational. You're letting your fear take control. No judge is going to give a man legal custody of an adult woman."

"But what if he does?" Her entire childhood swam before her eyes —out of control, in the clutches of an evil madman. She had fled that life and now it had caught up to her.

"He won't," Josh said confidently. Before she could argue, he continued speaking. "There are some things that trump custody, Sam."

"Like what? The fact that you're my employer? That won't mean anything."

"What if I'm your husband? No one will give someone custody of another man's wife."

Shock rendered her temporarily speechless, finally breaking through her terror. "Josh, that's...you can't...I appreciate your willingness to throw yourself on the sacrificial altar, but this is marriage. You can't do that."

"I can, and I will," he stubbornly insisted. With the resolution to marry her came something that felt a whole lot like relief, like a latch clicking into place after a long time of being stuck. Josh wanted to sigh with the liberation of the heavy weight he'd been under. Finally, after so many months of near torture the burden was gone. The tension between them had been unbearable. He'd thought it was because of their murky history and only now realized it was something else all together; they were attracted to each other, horribly and incurably. Now that he understood, now that he realized, he was almost glad to have the excuse to end their combined suffering. He was marrying Sam, and that was that. "Montana doesn't have a waiting period. We'll go today, get the license, and have a judge marry us." He stood and put down his hand for her. "Come on. Go change into a dress."

She stared at his hand. She had feared losing her mind, but somehow he sneaked past her and did it first. "You can't be serious."

"I am. Let's go; I want to get there before they close."

"Josh, you cannot do this. *We* can't do this. It's insane." She stared up at him with wild eyes, expecting to see the same level of crazy reflected in his gaze, but she didn't. His eyes were calm, placid, *resolved.*

"It's less insane than me killing that man, which is what I'm going to do if you don't do this."

"What?" she whispered.

"Do you think I would take the chance that he could ever hurt you again? That anyone could ever hurt you again? He hit you. He laid hands on you. That can never happen again. Marrying you is the best way to protect you. Short of that, I need to take him out of the equation. And he deserves it for what he did to you."

She pressed her palms to his cheeks. Now she was worried about him; he wasn't talking like a sane person. Something had gone seriously wrong with his brain. Josh, reasonable, rational Josh was gone; this new model was defunct and broken. "Josh, you can't kill a man. You'll go to prison."

"Then marry me and save me from jail."

Was he joking? He didn't look like he was, but with Josh sometimes it was difficult to tell. Why would he joke about this, though?

Josh wasn't exactly certain himself if he was being serious, at least about the killing someone part. He had never actually wanted to murder a man before, but then he had never heard anything as horrible as what Sam told him. The fact that her stepfather had preyed on her innocence was so repulsive he was afraid if he ever saw the man again he would make good on his threat and shoot him before he could blink.

All he could say for certain was he was desperate to do whatever it took to guarantee Sam's safety, and right now the best way looked like marriage. And maybe more than that he was merely desperate. Desperate for resolution, desperate for reprieve, desperate for *her*. She was too little, too vulnerable to be free floating in the world on her own. He had thought it before he ever heard of her stepfather. Sam needed a keeper, and he was well suited for the job. He would deal with any repercussions when they arose.

"You're really serious," she said after a few minutes of studying his unwavering expression. "You would really marry me." Her mouth was dry, eyes bulging. Not for the first time that day she felt like she might pass out. The shock of hearing him talk of marriage was somehow greater than the meaty fist she'd taken to her face.

"Don't you want to marry me?" he asked. For the first time a hint of vulnerability snaked into his tone. He dropped to his knees in front of her, putting them back at eye level.

"You know I do, Josh," she mumbled shyly. Unable to maintain eye contact any longer, her gaze dropped to her lap and her hands, now knotted together in an anxious tangle.

He wasn't sure why those words should cause a tidal wave of elation to open in his chest, but they did. He smiled at her and squeezed her hand, reaching out his free hand to tip her face back to his. "Then go change into a dress. I'll wear a suit. It will feel more like a wedding that way," he said softly. She blinked at him confused, shocked, but pretty, oh, so achingly pretty. Still smiling, he stood and pulled her up beside him. He put his hands on her shoulders and gave her a light shove in the direction of her room. "Quickly, we need to go."

She stumbled toward her room in a daze and pulled out one of her pretty new dresses, not allowing her mind to think any longer. After slipping the dress over her head, she stole into the bathroom and grimaced at the picture she presented. What good was a pretty dress if it went with a bruised and bloody face?

Carefully, she reapplied her makeup and rearranged her hair. If anyone looked closely, Sam's bruise was still apparent through her makeup, but for the most part she looked almost normal. Pretty, even. Was she glowing from excitement or nerves?

Josh didn't care what was making her look extra beautiful, only that she did. He had a difficult time tearing his eyes off her as they walked to the truck. He lifted her up, his hands lingering a moment at her waist as he gazed into her lovely, sweet face. Then he walked to his side of the truck and hopped in.

They didn't talk on the long trip to the city. They had to bypass their town because it had no courthouse or judge. All legal transactions had to be performed in the big city, which was two hours away.

Sam remained rooted to the spot as Josh parked the truck in front of the courthouse. He came around to lift her down, but she stopped him by once again cupping his cheeks and looking deeply into his eyes.

"Josh, you don't have to do this. Please take some time to think it through."

But Josh didn't want to think it through. He had spent his whole life overthinking everything. This once, he wanted to do what felt good. And at this moment, nothing would feel better than making Sam his. Her azure eyes pled with him, but they had the opposite effect of making him think rationally. All he could see was someone smashing his fist into those pretty eyes, bruising them. There was still a faint outline of blood in her nostril, and from this close up he could see the angry purple welt on her cheek.

His emotions broiled once again as he thought of the danger she had been in today and the damage that had already been inflicted on her. He felt a raging, desperate need to keep her safe, to make things right, and the only way his overheated mind could conjure was to make her legally his.

"Marry me, Sam," he whispered desperately. "Please be mine, really and truly mine." His voice was ragged, as were his emotions.

"I can't say no when you ask me like that," she said, sounding as tortured as she felt. "But I know you and I know when you return to sanity you're going to hate me for going along with this." She swiped at her brimming eyes. "This is torture." Should she do what was best for him and make him angry now, or should she do what he was telling her and make him angry later? She knew he was caught up in the heat of the moment. At any time, he would begin thinking clearly again, and he would realize what a mistake this was.

But then she selfishly thought about what *she* wanted. She wanted to be married to Josh. She loved him, and she could make him happy. They could work together. They had already proved they were a good team. And if she didn't marry him, she might leave him at the mercy of someone like Chelsea, someone who would use and destroy him. So what was best? Marrying him or not marrying him?

"Josh," she groaned. Then she leaned in and kissed him. If he had shrugged away or seemed repulsed, she would have had her answer. But he did neither of those things. Instead he responded wholeheartedly as if he'd been waiting for it, tugging her hips closer, wrapping her legs around his waist, and plastering her upper half against the seat as he returned the kiss with interest, plunging his fingers so deep in her hair they might never untangle. When that kiss was finished, he kissed her again and a third time until at last she pushed him away and straightened her disheveled skirt, gasping for air and a smidgen of sanity.

"All right, I'll marry you," despite her best efforts, she was still breathless.

He grinned at her, his lips lopsided and swollen with passion. "Because I'm a good kisser?"

"You're an amazing kisser," she said, shuddering with a little thrill of delighted expectation. She knew him better than anyone, and even she hadn't known he had a kiss like that inside him. Her Josh was ridiculously and over-the-top passionate. Who knew? "And because we've proved there's more than friendship between us," she said.

He lifted her down and took her hand, giving her an all-knowing Josh look. "I already knew there was. You could have asked me."

"My way was more fun," she said, aiming for prim and failing mightily when she reviewed their kiss.

Josh laughed and leaned in to bite her earlobe, whispering, "Good point."

They suspended conversation while they filled out the appropriate forms to get their license. Forty-five minutes after they arrived, they were sitting outside a judge's office waiting to be married. Josh held her small hand in both his big ones as they sat in the lobby, his fingers absently exploring the contours, and then it was their turn.

Sam's hand shook as they recited their vows; Josh's didn't. She kept darting him glances all throughout the short ceremony as if giving him the opportunity to renege, but he didn't. He resolutely repeated the appropriate words, sounding sure and joyful. Meanwhile Sam needed prompted a few times before she could get the words past her dry lips.

"We should get something to eat," Josh declared after the ceremony was over. "We're not going to feel like cooking when we get home."

Sam gulped. *Home.* The ranch was her home now, really and truly hers. She wondered how long it would take before she stopped feeling like an interloping stranger in the big, beautiful house.

They ate at a fast food hamburger joint. Josh was almost finished with his meal before he threw down what was left of his burger onto his plastic plate.

"What am I thinking? We can't eat here on our wedding day."

"We like it here," Sam said simply. "Why shouldn't we?"

"We should eat somewhere fancy, like a steakhouse."

"Do you think we're steakhouse people? We like the simple things in life, Josh. Who cares what we *should* do? Let's do what we want. It's our life. I like it here. They have a special sauce no steakhouse can duplicate."

He watched her as she licked a spot of said sauce from her thumb, his heart kicking into overdrive once more. He smiled. "You're cute, Samantha."

She startled and looked up at him in surprise. "Huh?" Beyond telling her she was smart and a capable ranch hand, he had never paid her a compliment before. "Am I dying or something?"

He leaned in, resting his chin in his hand as he inspected her. "You're my wife. I should probably start saying nice things to you."

"Your wife," she repeated. Then she clapped her hand over her mouth, sprinted to the bathroom, and threw up in the toilet.

CHAPTER 20

"You sure you're okay?" Josh asked for the dozenth time since they left the restaurant.

"I'm fine," Sam assured him, as she had every time he'd asked. Thankfully she always kept a toothbrush and paste in her purse. After brushing her teeth twice, she could only taste the minty effect of the toothpaste. Why was she the one panicking over their hasty nuptials? By all rights it should be Josh. After all, she was in love with him and had been since the day she met him two years ago. Up until very recently, he had loathed her. Maybe he still did. Maybe this was all part of some elaborate payback scheme.

Her thoughts were still in a whirl as they pulled up in front of the house. Once again, Sam remained rooted to the seat and didn't even move when Josh came to get her.

"Sam?" he asked. He hovered in the open passenger doorway. His finger lightly touched her knee, jolting her.

She turned to look at him, eyes wide with worry and trepidation. "Josh, there's something we need to discuss before we go inside."

"Yes?" he prompted, tone wary.

"I was wondering if this is supposed to be a marriage in name only." Rarely had she been so blunt, but she needed to know. Had he simply married her to give her the protection of the King name?

Josh, on the other hand, was amused by the question. "Samantha, have you ever known me to do anything halfheartedly?" He grabbed her ankles, yanked her closer, and kissed her, the same sort of toe curling kiss they'd shared before they left to get married, the kind that left her hair undone, that left *her* undone. She leaned against the seat for support, boneless, breathless, a shaky mess "Does that answer your question?" Josh asked when the steamy kiss had ended. He was uncharacteristically cocky now, but he couldn't seem to help it. Suddenly his brothers' cockiness made perfect sense; there was something to be said for leaving a woman in this condition, so high on his kisses she couldn't see straight, let alone breathe. Neither could he, but he was slightly better at covering.

Sam gripped his shirt with both hands, pulling him close enough to brush her lips on his when she spoke. "Almost, but I think I have further questions that might need more detailed answers inside."

He laughed and pulled her from the vehicle. Instead of setting her on the ground, he kept her cradled in his arms and carried her up the porch steps, unable to take his eyes off her. When had she gotten so beautiful, and how had he missed it for so long? She was lovely, and she was *his.* "Welcome home, Mrs. King," he said softly. Then he carried her over the threshold, closing the door decidedly behind them with his foot.

* * *

Saturdays were generally light work days at the ranch. Unless there was a special project, only the necessary daily chores were performed. Josh called Tanner in order to tell him he would be absent for those chores.

On Sunday, Josh and Sam skipped church.

But on Monday, there was no way either of them could skip out on their work.

"The honeymoon is over," Sam muttered, feeling like their happiness really was at an end.

"We should take a real honeymoon," Josh said, studying their joined hands as they lay twined together on his chest. She was so small, so fragile and in need of care. How had he ignored that for so long? *Never again,* he vowed. Sam would never be alone and unprotected for as long as he drew breath. "As soon as Cam and Belle come back and can cover some of the work here."

Sam had no reply to that. He had surprised her once again. All weekend she had waited for him to wake up and come to his senses, but he never had. At any moment, she expected him to look at her in surprise, having no idea why she was sleeping next to him in his bed, but that had never happened. Not that they'd done a lot of sleeping. They had been idyllically happy, deliriously so. But now the real world had to come calling.

They ate breakfast together like usual, this time holding hands over their bowls of cereal. Before he left he gave her a lingering kiss goodbye, pulling her into his lap and letting his hands have free reign on her body. *His wife.* He could hardly believe his good fortune.

"I'll see you later, baby girl," he whispered in a new tone that made her smile in anticipation, reluctantly drawing himself away after giving her a kiss—or ten—goodbye.

"Are you feeling better?" Ethan asked when he called Sam first thing that morning after Josh's departure.

She had no idea how to respond. While her stepfather had developed an elaborate series of lies to explain the injuries he gave her, Sam had never figured out a plausible way to explain her bruises.

"I had a bloody nose and a headache," she said at last. Both of those things were true.

"Wow, gross," Ethan said. "I thought maybe you were playing hooky to get ready for your visitors."

"My visitors?" she echoed.

"Uh-oh," Ethan said. "Either it was supposed to be a surprise, or someone forgot to tell you."

"Tell me what?"

He remained silent.

"Please, Ethan. If someone is coming here, I *need* to know."

He laughed. "Why, is the place a mess?"

"Something like that," she muttered.

"Okay, it's the parents."

"The parents," she repeated dully.

"You know, the Kings. Belle's a nervous wreck about it. I don't know why; she said they're perfectly nice. Between you and me, I think she completely forgot they were coming. Now she has to scramble her work here and try to get home tonight, too. Maybe people always freak out when their in-laws come to visit."

Apparently so because Sam was pretty sure she was experiencing her own freak out. For the rest of the day, her attention was divided. A part of her focused on her work and performed it conscientiously. The other part of her was having a panicked meltdown. In a few short hours, she was supposed to meet in-laws who had no idea she existed. What if they hated her? What if they didn't approve of the unplanned marriage? And, most distressing of all, how would Josh react to the sudden appearance of his parents?

If she had been able to foresee the answer to that question, her anxiety would have ratcheted up to cosmic levels.

* * *

FOR THE FIRST time in his life, Josh did not want to be at work. Usually he felt blessed because not only did he love his job, but he had been born into it. He hadn't had to go to school for years or work his way up a corporate ladder. He had been born the boss, but he didn't take that fact for granted, trying hard to work as much or more than his employees.

But today he wanted to go home to Sam, his wife. His *wife*. He still couldn't believe he had done something so impulsive, and yet it had worked out perfectly. If the last couple of days were any indication, he should base all his decisions on an emotional impulse and stop thinking so much.

He was whistling as he made his way back to the house that evening, then his eyes narrowed on an unfamiliar car in the driveway. It looked like a rental car. That was funny because the only rental cars they ever had were when his parents...

The thought broke off and died as he stared at the house. Oh, no. Oh, no, no, no. Before anyone at the house could catch sight of him, he hopped off his horse and ducked behind a barn, bending over to try and suck some air into his suddenly deflated lungs.

What had he done? In his entire whirlwind courtship of Sam, he hadn't given one thought to his family. Even Coy, who thus far had the most impulsive marriage, had taken Ivy to Arizona to meet their parents. Yet he, Josh, who had always been the most fastidious brother, had married a stranger. A stranger he supposedly despised. And they would never let him live it down. Furthermore no one in town would ever believe he and Sam hadn't had something going on two years ago when she was pretending to be a man.

How was he supposed to see his parents, the parents who had trusted him enough to let him remain with his brothers at the tender age of sixteen, and tell them he had married a stranger on a whim?

I know you'll be a good boy and do the right thing, Josh; you always do. Those had been his mother's parting words to him when she moved away from the ranch four years ago, and now he had let her down and broken her trust, possibly irrevocably. There was no way to undo what he had done, and he didn't want to. He was happy he married Sam. He had simply gone about things the wrong way. His parents would love Sam when they got to know her. The problem was they didn't know her at all.

He stood upright and tried to draw a deep breath around the anxiety that had squeezed his lungs like an accordion. That was it; that was the key. He would convince Sam they needed to keep their marriage a secret until they could ease the rest of the family into it. His parents would meet Sam and they would love her, who didn't? He would pretend to transition into a dating relationship with her to get them used to the idea of her. Then, in a few months when he was certain they were comfortable with the idea of her, he would announce that they had been married for some time already. Unless he could convince Sam to undergo another church ceremony. Then he would never have to own up to his baffling, impulsive behavior. He would talk to Sam about it and see which she thought was the best course of action. She had good ideas; she could help him figure out what to do.

Feeling slightly cheered, he grasped his horse's reins and headed for the house.

* * *

SAM WASN'T sure what to do. She heard the car doors slam, but no one else was home. Should she go out and welcome the older couple to their own home? Should she introduce herself as their new daughter-in-law? No, definitely not. That was a no-brainer; she would wait for Josh to drop that bomb.

The ranch was too remote for her to pretend she hadn't heard them. She stood and made her way down the hall, nervously smoothing imaginary wrinkles from her pants. Though she had heard a car door open and close a while ago, they hadn't entered the house. When she stepped onto the porch, she saw why.

She knew Josh's father had a crippling case of rheumatoid arthritis. It was the reason they had moved to Arizona four years ago. The dry heat was easier for his painful, aching joints. But when Sam tried to picture him, she hadn't counted on how the disease would mangle him, deforming his limbs until they looked like gnarled tree branches. Fingers that used to bend down now twisted up. Even though she knew he wasn't yet sixty, as his wife helped him from the car, Sam saw a weathered, crippled old man who was bent over two canes and barely able to hobble.

He was smiling, though, and looked cheerful despite the painful disease. He stood as straight as he was able and took in a deep breath, closing his eyes and appearing to savor the country air.

Sam hugged a porch beam with one arm, feeling suddenly shy and intrusive for observing this private moment of homecoming. The couple, sensing her presence, turned to her with a smile.

"You must be Sam," Mrs. King said.

"Yes, ma'am," Sam said shyly. Reluctantly, she let go of the porch beam and made her way down the porch steps, her arm outstretched to shake hands. But when she reached Mrs. King, the older woman pulled her into a hug.

"It's so nice to meet you. We've heard so many nice things about you."

From whom? Sam wanted to ask. Certainly not from Josh, that much she knew.

"So they've got you working for Belle and you haven't run away screaming yet," Mr. King said. "You must have a lot of grit."

Sam laughed. "You should see her at her office in New York. I'm pretty sure she made a guy in a cubicle cry by looking at him."

The Kings laughed and then, as if by magic, some other family members began to filter toward them.

"Hey, Mom and Dad," Coy said. Ivy trailed behind him and Sam stood back while hugs were traded all around. Cade appeared in the office and began to roll himself toward the fray. Far away, Layla stepped out of their house and began to jog toward the gathering.

When everyone was gathered and talking, creating a cacophony of noise, Josh appeared around the corner of the barn, leading his horse. As if everyone knew there was about to be a momentous announcement, all conversation came to a halt as everyone turned to stare expectantly at the youngest brother. Sam clasped her hands nervously behind her back, as if she were a soldier at ease, although she felt anything less than at ease.

"Hey, Mom and Dad," Josh said with forced cheerfulness. "What are you doing here?"

"Joshua King, how could you forget that your dad and I always visit this same time every year?"

"I've had a lot going on," Josh said sheepishly.

"You're not the only one who forgot," his father said. "Cam and Belle had to scramble their plans and hop a flight home at the last minute. I told them to stay there, but they said they wanted us all to be together."

"Hmm," Josh said. Sam thought he looked and sounded nervous. She wanted to move closer to him and draw comfort, but he hadn't yet looked at her or made a move in her direction. Was he going to wait for Cam and Belle to get here before he shared the news?

Then he looked at her, and she knew. He had no plans to tell anyone anything. Reality had finally sunk in; sanity had finally returned. As she knew would happen when he finally came to his senses, he was emotionally backpedaling and regretting their marriage.

Her eyes filled with tears and she turned away to hide them. "I'll make us some iced tea," she said before quickly scurrying into the house.

She barely made it to the kitchen before she broke down. Grabbing a dishtowel, she pressed it to her face and wept, wincing slightly when she pressed against her bruise. How could she have been so stupid to think there would be a happily ever after for her? Would Josh want a divorce? An annulment? A time machine? How else could he pretend nothing had happened between them but to go back and erase it?

If only this had happened two days ago before their perfect weekend, she wouldn't have blamed him. If he had thrown up his hands in the judge's office and said, "What am I doing? I can't marry you," she would have understood. But why did he put her through the anguish of making her feel loved and cherished and then take that away? Was he really that heartless?

More importantly, what was she supposed to do now that she was trapped in the house with a husband who didn't want her and a family who didn't know she existed?

CHAPTER 21

Somehow Sam pulled herself together. Making tea helped give her a purpose as well as something to do with her hands. While it was steeping, she went down the hall and tried to remove all traces of her tears.

The waterworks had rubbed off her earlier makeup, causing her fading cheek bruise to show through. She covered that, dabbed at her eyes, and pressed a cool compress to them.

When she exited the room, the family was crammed into the kitchen. Sam finished the task of making her iced tea by pivoting around family members and Cade's wheelchair as they talked and laughed together. She felt Josh's eyes on her, but she dared not look at him for fear of losing control again. She was immensely thankful for the other wives and brothers who kept the attention off her, allowing her to stand in the background and soak up the stories. Josh stood on the other side of the kitchen, smiling blandly, his arms crossed over his chest. Every once in a while he looked at her and frowned, trying to catch her eye.

Just as she feared attention was about to turn in her direction, Cam and Belle arrived home and the frenzy began again.

Layla, bless her, had made supper for everyone so the party

trekked to her house. Sam flitted about the kitchen doing Layla's bidding, once again thankful for something to do.

Finally it was time for supper. Sam ended up sitting across from Josh. She felt like Mr. and Mrs. King were watching them, looking for any hint things had thawed between them. No doubt they were well acquainted with the story of their rocky relationship. Who wasn't?

Josh touched her foot with his under the table, but she quickly jerked her foot away before thinking better and giving a swift kick to his shin. He grunted and hunched over his plate, rubbing his shin.

"What's wrong with you?" Cade asked him.

"She kicked me," he scowled at Sam.

Sam was mortified that he had ratted her out, but Mr. King laughed and used his napkin to try and keep his food from blowing out his mouth.

"If there's one thing I learned raising four boys, it's that occasionally they need a good swift kick now and then," Mrs. King said unconcernedly.

"Does that mean I can kick her back?" Josh asked irritably.

"If you want one of your brothers to break your legs," his mother returned sweetly.

Sam thought she was going to like her new mother-in-law very much.

After supper, the family trekked back to the main house because it was roomier for visiting, and because the brothers had to help their parents unload their belongings from the car.

"Sam, you sit here by me," Mrs. King said. "I want to get to know you a little bit." Sam sat beside her, wondering what she could possibly say that wouldn't reveal her inner emotional turmoil. "You have such lovely, unique features. I would love to paint you sometime."

Art seemed like a safe topic, so Sam fastened on it. "You paint? I didn't know."

"It's my passion," Mrs. King said. She turned to look over her shoulder at Belle. "Belle, dear, that reminds me. I've finally finished your wedding portrait. It's that one there, Cam, the wrapped canvas."

"I can't wait to see it, Mom," Cam said enthusiastically. He stood and dove for the canvas, eagerly unwrapping it. Everyone else stood and surrounded him and Belle in a semi-circle. At first, Sam was certain what she saw was a joke and the real painting would be revealed momentarily, but then everyone ooh-ed and ahh-ed, so she knew she was looking at the real thing, but it looked nothing like Cam and Belle, if that was who it was supposed to be.

In real life, Cam's hair was almost blond, like Josh's. In the painting, it was liberally streaked with black. But he got off lightly in his representation compared to Belle. For some reason, she was very red. Her skin tone was almost the color of a fire truck. Her eyes were crossed, her lips puckered like a fish, and her arms were so long that if they were real they would hang to her shins. With maximum effort, Sam refrained from laughing hysterically.

"Oh, honey, look at it," Cam said.

"I can't not look at it. It's so...I look...I really...I can't believe it," Belle said at last. "Wow. It's really something, Lori."

"Do you want me to hang it on the mantel right now?" Cam asked. He made a move toward the fireplace, throwing a mischievous smile to Belle over his shoulder.

"Yes I do," she replied. "The one in our bedroom, of course, so I can see it first thing every morning. I want to keep it as close as possible." She threw Cam a look that promised retribution later.

"Isn't that sweet," Mrs. King said. Her happy smile looked genuine, but from the painting it was difficult for Sam to believe the older woman didn't hate Belle. Why else had she made her look like a red tree sloth?

Thankfully, attention never returned to Sam again. The older Kings were tired from their trip, and everyone turned in early. Once again Josh tried to catch Sam's attention by motioning outside toward the porch, but she ignored him and went to her room, trying hard not to slam the door.

After her nighttime routine, she crawled between the sheets, closed her eyes, and let her pent-up tears flow. Beside her, the bed bowed, alerting her to Josh's presence. He reached for her and drew her to his chest. At first, his touch felt so good and so comforting she gave in without a thought. Then reality returned with a vengeance and she shoved away from him.

"What are you doing here?" she hissed.

"What do you mean what am I doing here? We're married."

"We are? Then why are we the only people who know about it?" She hopped out of bed and strode toward the door.

Josh remained in the bed, scowling at her. "Why do you think? I can't spring something like that on them. I think we should ease them into it."

Sam's hands clenched at her sides. "Really? And how do you propose doing that?"

He should have been alerted by her overly calm, patronizing tone, but he wasn't. He plunged in blindly, laying out his plan.

"So, to recap, you want to pretend we're getting along now. Then, in a little while, you want us to pretend to date. Once you're sure everyone has accepted the idea of us as a couple you'll gently break the news of our marriage, possibly in a few months. But in the mean time, you'll still stay with me at night, reserving the full benefits of our secret marriage."

"Yeah," he said, nodding his head like the enthusiastic idiot he was.

"Out. Get out." For emphasis, she jabbed her finger toward the door.

"What?" He stared at her, incredulous, distracted by the pretty picture she presented in her white see-through nightie.

"I said get out of my room."

He stood and advanced on her. "Sam, be reasonable. I can't go back to the way it was before. That's crazy."

"Crazy? Crazy is pretending your wife is a stranger. If you think you can ignore me all day and sneak in here like I'm some sort of lady of the night to be used by you, you are sorely mistaken. Unless and until you are ready to tell your family about us, consider yourself single." She opened the door and nudged him through it by using her hand on his chest.

Now he was angry. His lips pinched together in a tight line. "I'm not going to tell them until I think they're ready to hear it."

"Good, have fun sleeping alone." She closed the door in his face and locked it for good measure.

He wanted to pound his fists on it until she either opened it or he knocked it down. Then he would talk to her and make her see reason. He was certain that if she simply gave it some time, she would see things his way.

Instead, he returned to his room, grumpy and irritable. Now he understood some of Solomon's proverbs about wives. What was wrong with her? Why couldn't she see things from his perspective? His idea would work to her benefit, too. If they did things his way, neither of them would lose face. They would lessen the chance of being fodder for the gossip mill. He was sure that, given time, Sam would come around. He simply had to be patient and wait for her to become rational.

CHAPTER 22

Sam supposed it was some small comfort that Josh didn't regret marrying her; he simply regretted the way their marriage came about. But she also knew if she gave in to him now, she would spend the rest of her life bowing to his pride. She wanted, no, *needed* for him to be the one to break first. As much as she missed him, she was even angrier with him. And she was hurt.

From his point of view, he didn't want to hurt his parents by announcing that he had married a stranger without their blessing. But from Sam's point of view, his refusal to go public said he was ashamed and embarrassed by her. She expected to face some flack over their hasty nuptials, but she assumed they would take their lumps together. After all, if they presented a united front, they could endure anything. Since meeting his parents, she didn't think they would object to the marriage. They might be disappointed they hadn't been there for the ceremony. If that were the case, Sam had no problem having a church wedding in town.

But she absolutely refused to pretend the marriage had never happened, at least not to Josh. If he wanted to live in some la-la land where he covered his mistakes by pretending they didn't exist, so be it. She had no plans to live there with him.

The next morning the atmosphere between them was arctic. She was glad his parents and Belle and Cam were there to help cover the tension. Belle and Cam were only staying a few days, but the Kings would be staying for two weeks. Sam had no idea what would happen after they left if she and Josh hadn't resolved their standoff. And if this morning's icy silence was any indication, there would be no resolution any time soon.

After the men left for the day, Mrs. King busied herself in the kitchen. She had volunteered to cook supper that night. Sam was torn between wanting to help her and doing the job for Belle that she was paid to do. Thankfully, Mrs. King sensed her dilemma and hastened to help her out of it.

"I know you ladies have a lot of work to do in the office today. It must have been difficult for you to arrange the time off, Belle. I'm sure you would appreciate Sam's help getting caught up with your work."

"I would, thank you," Belle said. She and Sam closeted themselves in the office and, as before when Belle had been home, the day was a whirlwind of activity. Belle could have been featured in one of those army commercials because she did more in one morning than most people did in a week. This morning, however, Sam almost outpaced her in what she accomplished. Never before had working felt so good. She only wished she had somewhere to escape to this evening so she wouldn't have to be surrounded by her new family who had no idea they were her new family.

"Everything okay, Sam?" Belle asked.

For one wild moment, Sam was tempted to confess to her new sister-in-law. Then the phone rang, distracting them from any personal talk, and the busy day started up again.

"Belle, sweetheart, supper's ready." Cam stood in the doorway and studied his wife with a smile.

She returned his smile and stood.

"Are you feeling okay?" Cam asked, his smile changing to a frown.

"I feel fine," Belle said warily. "Why?"

"You're looking a little red." He grasped her hands. "Is it my imagination, or have your arms grown?"

Sam sputtered a laugh that turned into a hysterical fit of giggles. Ever since she saw the horrible painting the night before, she had been dying to release the laughter building inside her. Now she turned away and hid her mouth in her elbow to try and quiet her gut-wrenching laughter.

"Now look what you've done; you've broken Sam. She's too little to laugh that hard. Her body probably doesn't have the energy to support so much movement," Belle said, making Sam laugh harder.

"If you think ours is bad, you should see the one of Coy and Ivy. She looks like a cornstalk. Our theory is it's our mom's passive-aggressive way of working out her daughter-in-law angst."

Sam doubled over, no longer attempting to keep her laughter in check. After everything that had happened yesterday with Josh it felt wonderful to laugh.

"Mom sent me to see what's taking so long," Josh said glumly from the doorway. "What's wrong with her?"

"It's called laughter," Cam explained. "Try it sometime."

Sam had to perch on the edge of the chair in order to avoid toppling to the floor. She couldn't seem to get herself under control, and then her laughter changed to tears. Thankfully, Cam and Belle made a quiet exit, leaving her alone with Josh.

He entered the room and sat beside her, drawing her close and holding her while she cried.

"Sam, baby, please don't be sad. I'm not doing this because of you. I swear it. I'm happy we're married, honest." His hand smoothed gently up and down her spine, soothing her in spite of her lingering sadness.

"If you're so happy, why don't you tell people? Why hide it like it's a shameful secret?"

"Because I don't want to be laughed at again."

She eased away from him and wiped her eyes. "You mean like you were before when you found out about me?"

He nodded.

"Isn't that what this is really about, Josh? You're still angry at me, and this is your way of getting back at me."

"That's not true," he said vehemently. He had forgiven her the moment he learned she had dressed as a man in order to hide from her stepfather.

"I think it is," she insisted. "And you know what else? I don't care if people laugh because they'll be laughing at *us*. It's not only you anymore. We can be a team, we can stand together and say we don't care that people tease us about getting married so quickly. It doesn't have to be like this." Her pretty eyes were pleading, making it difficult to stay resolute, but he had spent many more years with his pride than he had with her.

"No. This is the way it has to be. I won't have people gossiping about us again. You have no idea what it was like."

"Don't I?" she snapped. "Don't you think I got the same thing? The same looks, winks, and nudges about all that time we spent alone together? But I didn't care because I knew the truth of what was between us. People are always going to talk, Josh. People are always going to look for something to laugh over or find fault with. The only thing you can control is your reaction to it."

"No, I can control my actions. I have a reputation to maintain."

"The only reputation you have is of an unforgiving, hard-nosed man, and you've worked very hard to maintain it these two years," she said. She stood. "You have a choice; you can have your pride and be alone, or you can have your wife and be happy, but there's not room enough in your life for both of us."

"What are you saying?" he asked.

"I think you know. I love you, I've always loved you, since the first day I met you, but I won't live my life hiding behind the shadow of your ego." With as much dignity as she could muster, she raised her head and walked from the room.

Was she really saying she would leave him if he didn't give in and do things her way? Once again his old friend anger returned to keep him company. If that was how she was going to be, then forget about her. If the marriage ended, no one would ever have to know it took place to begin with. He had never believed in divorce as an option, but right now it seemed much better than giving in and letting a woman rule his life. No way, no how would a girl call the shots for Joshua King.

With that thought in mind, he also stood and walked to the kitchen, and he didn't glance at Sam for the rest of the evening.

CHAPTER 23

*O*nce again Sam couldn't sleep. She kept replaying the scene with Josh in her head. Had she been too harsh? She hadn't intended mentioning an end to their marriage. She had simply been trying to grab his attention, but threatening to leave felt wrong. If they ever made up, she promised herself she would never do it again. There was too much at stake to use walking away as a bargaining chip. If they were going to be in it, they were going to be in it completely and forever.

With that decided, she began to doze until she heard a small sound from outside. Barely discernable, it was noticeable only because it was different from the normal night sounds. Creeping to her window, she peeked through her blinds and what she saw froze her heart.

The rustlers were back. The same truck and trailer were parked in front of Ivy's corral. Two men stood trying to open the gate with a sturdy-looking pair of bolt cutters. Another glint of metal alerted her to the fact that one of the men had a gun tucked in the front waistband of his pants. Sam felt almost dizzy with panic. That gun could only mean they were willing to use it on anyone who tried to stop them.

She debated with herself for a split second about what to do. If she alerted Josh, he would no doubt rush outside and might get himself killed. Of course she would call the sheriff, but he was an hour away. The thieves could be long gone by then. She couldn't let them get away, but what could she do?

Before she could make up her mind, the front door opened. She watched with horror as Josh bolted off the porch and ran at the two men, his rifle raised. She didn't stay to watch anymore. Instead, she darted out of her room, passing Mrs. King on the way.

"Call the sheriff and your other sons," Sam threw over her shoulder, and then she was outside. There was no light outside, but she could barely make out two men wrestling on the ground. If Josh didn't know one of them had a gun, and if he was able to reach it… No, she couldn't allow her mind to go down that path.

Josh's gun had been dropped during the struggle. Another man began lurching toward it as if he were dazed and injured. Sam jumped off the porch and grabbed the gun from the ground. She had terrible aim. If she fired, she might hit Josh, and the kickback would no doubt knock her down. Instead she turned it around so the barrel was facing her and used the butt end to hit the robber upside the head.

Already dazed, he fell to the ground unconscious. Sam stepped over him and walked toward Josh. Even through the darkness it was easy to see which one he was because he wasn't wearing a shirt. He and the other man rolled over and over, grunting with the effort it took to try and subdue each other. Sam thought Josh must realize the man had a gun and that was why he was trying to pin his arms, to keep him from reaching it.

She stood over them and raised the gun, waiting for an opportunity to bash the guy in the head when suddenly one of his hands worked free and grabbed for his gun. As if time stood still, she watched in slow motion as he pulled the weapon from his waistband and saw her towering over him with a gun. There was no time to scream before he raised it and fired. At her. She looked at Josh, saw him look at her in horror, then everything went black as she fell to the ground.

* * *

SOMEHOW, even after seeing Sam shot not two feet away from him, Josh was able to return his attention to the man beneath him. He slugged him so hard across the jaw he heard bone crack and he had no idea if it was his hand or the man's face. Either way the effect was the same. The man became immobile, the gun dropping from his slack hand.

Coy and Cam ran up to the scene then. Coy began securing the other man who was beginning to rally while Cam took both guns and checked on the man who had shot Sam. Josh couldn't have cared less about either of the men. His only goal was getting to Sam and forcing her to open her eyes and say she was fine, that the bullet had missed her.

But when he crawled over to her, the seeping wetness at his knees alerted him to the fact that she wasn't fine, the bullet hadn't missed her, and she was bleeding profusely.

"Help," Josh called. "Someone help." He looked at her and panicked, which was something he had never done before in the face of an emergency.

"Find the wound and press your hand on it." The steady voice of his father coached him from somewhere to his left.

"How can I find the wound?" Josh asked.

"Find where the blood is coming from," his father said.

Josh lifted her shirt and swiped at the ocean of blood with his hand, trying to see where it was spouting from. His head swam when he realized it was coming from her chest. What if the bullet had hit her heart? There was no way she would make it. He pressed his hand to the wound.

"Sam, can you hear me? Please say something. Please." He used as much pressure as he dared, trying to stem the flow of blood.

"Don't try to call her back to this, son," his father said. "Let her stay out; it's better for her to be unconscious right now."

In his mind, he knew that was true, but he was desperate for some reassurance that she was still with him. Still, his father was right. He switched to pleading with her in his mind. *Please Sam, please, please, please. Don't leave me. Please. Stay with me.*

He had never felt more helpless. All he could do was hold his hand on her and wait. His only comfort was the pulsing sensation of the blood spurting between his fingers, signaling that she was still alive. But after losing so much blood, how could she continue to remain that way? And the hospital was over an hour away by ambulance. There was no way she could make it, no way.

He was too dazed to realize the whirring sound he was hearing wasn't his own panicked heartbeat. A helicopter landed in a field beside the house and medical personal ran toward him. They moved him aside and began working on Sam.

He sat on his knees, watching them work on her while her blood dried on his hands. Absently, he scratched at them, but he didn't feel it. The moment took on a surreal tone as they put her on a gurney and carried her to the helicopter. As the blades began to turn, Josh had the strange feeling that he would never see her again.

With an anguished cry that was more of a moan, he dropped his head in his hands and started to weep.

* * *

AFTER THAT, things became even more of a chaotic blur. Cam called the charter company he and Belle used for their leer jet and rented a helicopter to fly Josh to the airport. Someone had to go with him, and for whatever reason, Coy was elected. The rest of the family would be traveling by car.

As soon as the helicopter was in the air, Josh realized why Coy had been the one sent with him. His brother put his arms around him and allowed him to cry on his chest like a baby. Cam wouldn't have been comfortable with such an emotional display from another man, and Cade wouldn't have been able to fit in the chopper with his wheelchair.

"You love her," Coy said, resting his head comfortingly on Josh's. It was a statement and not a question.

"Yes," Josh said between great hiccupping sobs that wracked his whole body.

They arrived at the hospital only a few minutes behind Sam. Coy went to the desk to enquire and Josh was jolted back to that day two years ago when he had taken her to a hospital. And then he had left her, sick and broken, to fend for herself. All because she had wounded his blasted pride.

"She's still in triage," Coy said. "I don't know how long that will take, but they'll come tell us when they have an assessment of her condition. Are you cold?"

"No," Josh said, but it sounded like a question. Why would he be cold? Then he looked down and realized he was wearing a pair of pajama pants and nothing else. Not only that, but his torso was covered in dried blood. And he was shivering violently. "Maybe I am. I don't know."

"I'll find you something." Coy left again, returning a few minutes later with a pair of scrubs. "They said there's a shower you can use."

"I don't want to leave," Josh said. He looked up at Coy with the same heartbreaking, mutinous expression he had used when he was a little boy and trying to buck Coy's authority.

Coy swallowed down a lump of emotion. "I'll come get you in the shower if there's any news. I promise. You need to get cleaned up. You don't want to look like that when you see her."

"Okay," Josh said numbly. He felt like his mind and body had been dosed with Novocain. He also knew when the feeling wore off, he was going to be in a whole lot of pain.

A kindly nurse showed him the way to the showers and pointed on the wall toward the combination soap and shampoo. Josh intended to take the world's fastest shower, but when the hot water hit him, he realized he was indeed cold. He stood under the spray until the violent shivering of his body stopped, and then he washed everything a couple of times, scrubbing hard to get the blood out. If only the memories were so easy to erase.

The scrubs were comfortable, if overly large. Absently he wondered which giant they belonged to. He was a big man, over six feet and broad shouldered; for something to be large on him meant the owner had to be huge.

When he returned to the sitting room, his family was there. Either they broke land/speed records to get there, or he was in the shower for longer than he thought. Before he found out, a doctor dressed similarly in scrubs stepped out from behind the swinging doors and made his way over to them.

"You brought in the gunshot wound," he said. "The bullet hit her spleen and liver and nicked a few other things. She's extremely critical and we need to operate now, but we'll need consent from her next of kin."

At first everyone looked in bewilderment at each other. How could they possibly find Sam's family when she was apparently alone in the world?

"That's me," Josh said, sitting up in alarm. *Surgery? Critical? Nicked her what?* "She's my wife."

The doctor nodded. "I'll send some papers for you to sign," he said, then turned and disappeared the way he came.

The silence left in his wake was deafening until Coy spoke.

"Oh, wow."

"Your wife," Cam said, eyes narrowed as he stared at Josh. "Did you say that so they would operate?"

Josh took a breath and turned to face the music. Amazing how little he cared about their reaction now. "No. Sam and I are married."

"Since when?" Belle asked.

"Since Friday."

"Why didn't you say anything?" This came from his mother.

"Because I'm an idiot and if I've lost her then it's nothing more than what I deserve." He sat and hung his head in his hands again. Thankfully this time his eyes remained dry, but he almost wished for tears. Anything would be better than this agonizing regret.

Ivy and Layla sat on either side of him, flanking him as a signal that all questions were at an end for a while. Josh had had enough.

CHAPTER 24

For ten hours, Josh's life hung in the balance along with Sam's because that's how long her surgery took. And when it was over, she still wasn't out of the woods.

They moved her to a post-surgery intensive care unit. Josh wasn't allowed to stay with her, but he was allowed to visit her every couple of hours. He did, as often as he could, each time having to re-prepare himself for the sight of her hooked to so many tubes and machines. Even her face was unrecognizably swollen from all the fluids they were pumping into her. She was in a coma, but he talked to her anyway while he gently smoothed his fingers along her arm.

Twenty four hours later, she was a little farther from death's door. There could still be complications, and she was till in a coma, but he could breathe a little easier. He could take another shower and eat some food without feeling so much panicked desperation.

The next day, her vital signs were better than expected. They moved her to a regular room and downgraded her condition from "critical" to "serious." Because she was out of the intensive care unit, she was allowed to receive visitors. His family took turns stopping in to say hello or to relieve him from his vigil.

The following day another visitor showed up unexpectedly.

"Hey, is it okay if I come in?" Chelsea said, poking her head around the corner.

"Okay," Josh drawled. He was surprised to realize she felt like a stranger to him. How was it possible she had once been his dream? After everything he had been through with Sam, his relationship with Chelsea seemed empty and hollow, like shallow fluff.

"How are you holding up?" Chelsea asked.

"Okay," Josh repeated.

"We were all so shocked to hear Leo and his cousin were responsible for this." That was true; Leo had never mentioned he was planning to steal from the Kings. Though if he had, Chelsea probably would have found it amusing. "I can't believe his cousin shot her." She rubbed her hands together, trying to gather enough nerve for her last-ditch, desperate plan. "Josh, do you remember how I told you I saw Sam and Leo together?"

He scowled. "That wasn't true."

"Well, I was thinking: what if they were in on it together all along?"

He blinked at her. Was she insane? What was she talking about? "Then why would they shoot her?"

"To keep her quiet?" she guessed.

"Then why would she hit one of them in the head and raise a gun at the other one to try and save my life?"

Chelsea licked her suddenly dry lips. "Well, maybe, um, she panicked too, and, uh…"

He raised his hand. "Stop, just stop. As a matter of fact, please leave. I don't ever want to hear another word about my wife from your lips."

"Your wife," she choked. "You're married?"

He didn't respond.

"You could get it annulled," she said weakly.

He stood.

Realizing she had pushed things too far and he cared about Sam much more than she realized, Chelsea stood and scurried from the room as Lizzie and Tanner entered.

"Was that Chelsea?" Tanner asked. "Are you two back together?"

"What?" Josh asked, sinking into his chair once again. "No, never."

"Whew," Tanner said, making an exaggerated motion of wiping sweat from his brow. "Thank goodness."

"You never mentioned you didn't like her," Josh said.

"No offense, Josh, but you're not one much for constructive criticism. But now that it's over, I should tell you that she cheated on you. A lot."

"What?" Josh said, blinking at his foreman in shock.

Tanner nodded. "She's one of those girls who, if her lips are moving, then she's lying."

Lizzie nodded her agreement. "He's right, you know. I don't even know her, but I know a lot about her. She has an, uh, interesting reputation in town."

"You don't know her?" Josh asked, remembering how Chelsea told him Lizzie had said horrible things about him and Sam.

"No, I've never talked to her before. I thought she was dating Leo. I saw them making out a few weeks ago in his truck." She froze. "Please tell me you weren't together then."

"We were," Josh said. He stared at Sam lying motionless in the bed. For so long Chelsea had been his dream and ideal. He had held Sam at arm's length, accusing her of being a liar. But all along he had them mixed up. Sam was his dream; Chelsea wouldn't know the truth if it came up and introduced itself to her. He smiled, leaned forward, and rested his forehead against Sam's temple. "I love you, Mrs. King. Please wake up."

"Um, somehow the gossip mill has missed something," Tanner said. "I'm confused."

Josh sat back and told them the whole story. It didn't seem so bad when he said it out loud to them. In fact, it sounded rather romantic. And if there reaction was anything like the town's would be, they thought it was sweet rather than scandalous. As he relayed the story, he realized he needed to make amends to Sam in a very big way. And as his story came to an end, he had a very big idea.

* * *

SAM FELT GROGGY. Wait, was groggy the right word? She felt like she was stuck between wakefulness and sleep. There was something pulling her toward the conscious world, but she didn't know what it was.

Then she heard him; Josh said something and laughed. Josh. She needed to see Josh.

She didn't realize she had murmured his name out loud until he was leaning down beside her. "Sam? Sweetheart, are you awake?"

She tried to blink, but her eyes wouldn't work. "Maybe," she muttered. "Things aren't working so good." Was her tongue working? Had he understood that?

Apparently so, if his chuckle was any indication. "Take your time. You've been out a long while."

"How long?" she asked.

"Six days," he replied.

"Happy anniversary," she murmured, and then she was out again.

When she woke a few hours later, it was the same day. She knew because Josh was still there, talking to her as he coaxed her to open her eyes and come fully awake, his hand making soothing passes on her forehead, his smile a little soggy, a little sappy as he stared at her face.

Using all of her will and effort, she forced herself to slowly drag her eyes open. Thankfully, he had remembered to dim the lights. Still, she blinked against the soft glow and licked her dry lips.

"Did I hit Leo in the head, or was that a dream?"

"You gave him a concussion," Josh said proudly. "And I broke his cousin's jaw, nose, and three teeth."

"Did you hurt your hand?" She tried to focus on his hand, but saw hers instead. "What's that?" She tried to lift her hand, but it wouldn't cooperate.

"That's your ring," he said. He lifted her hand and held it up for her inspection. It was a huge diamond set in platinum, surrounded by several smaller diamonds.

"You bought me a ring?" she said, confused.

"It matches mine." He showed her his platinum band.

"But then people will know we're married."

"Everyone knows already," he said.

"Are you okay with that?" she asked tentatively.

He smiled. "I want to show you something." On her nightstand was their hometown paper. It was barely eight pages long, but still published a daily edition. Josh reached for it and opened it to the back. Before her was a picture of her and Josh from their trip to New York, smiling, happy, and huge because the picture took up an entire page, along with the words. "Josh King married Sam McCoy because he loves her and for no other reason."

Sam swallowed hard and gazed slowly around the room. "Am I dead?"

"No, thank goodness," Josh said. "Are you ready for a little light?"

"I guess," Sam said. Josh walked to the window and opened the blind. Across the street was a giant billboard with the same picture and ad on it.

"Josh," she started, but he interrupted her. "Wait, there's one more thing." He opened a laptop and pushed a button. A news story popped up from a popular daily broadcast from New York. There Sam saw the same billboard, and then the camera flashed to an interview with Josh standing outside what she could only assume was the hospital.

"So you took out these ads for your wife, even though she's in a coma," the reporter said.

"Yes, but she's expected to wake up soon, and I wanted her to know I'm glad I married her."

"From all accounts, it was a hasty marriage."

"The marriage was quick, but the courtship wasn't. She's been my best friend for the last couple of years, and I've loved her for most of it."

The reporter wished him luck, and the story ended.

"Josh," Sam said. "Are you crazy?"

"After this week, yes." He gathered her hands in his and kissed them. "Don't ever do that to me again, Sam. I thought I was going to lose you."

"Are you saying this because I'm sick and still might die?" she asked.

"No. After seeing you survive two horrific accidents, I'm beginning to think you have supernatural death-defying powers, but I'm not willing to test the theory a third time. I'm saying this because I love you, and I want you to know. I've loved you so long I don't know when I started to love you. I want everyone to know. I've been a hard-hearted fool, too stubborn and proud to know what's good for me, and I almost lost you because of it. I'm sorry. Please don't leave me, Sam. Please stay and work it out. I can't lose you at this stage of the game, or ever, really. You're my girl," he added, sounding shy and vulnerable as he stopped speaking and waited for her reply.

"I'm sorry I threatened you with leaving," Sam said. With effort, she lifted her hand to brush the hair off his forehead and cup his cheek. "I would never leave you, Josh. You're my husband. You're my best friend." She paused. "I do have one request, though."

"Anything," he promised.

"When I'm better, I want my old job back. I want to work on the ranch with you."

He thought how amazing it would be to have Sam at his side again, but as his wife this time. "But, Sam, you're recovering from a gunshot wound. I don't want to take any chances with your health."

Sam drew him closer until he was in the bed beside her, then she snuggled up next to him when he put his arm around her. "Would you believe me if I told you working for Belle takes more energy and stamina than a day in the saddle roping steers?"

He laughed, but before he could answer, she was once again asleep.

*E*xactly one year later, Layla finally found a new project.

"Twins," Coy said to Cade. "I can't believe you had twins. You're not a twin; that's not fair."

"Any of us could have twins," Cam pointed out.

"Not us," Belle said. "We're having one baby at a time, thank you very much."

"Put in your order now, sweetheart, I'm pretty sure that's how it works," Cam said.

Belle stared at the baby boy sleeping peacefully in her arms. "Although this really isn't so bad. He's actually much cuter and sweeter than I thought he would be." The baby opened his eyes and started to cry, and Belle looked around in panic. "Take it, somebody take it, quick."

Josh reached out and took his nephew. He had seen Belle drop one too many cartons of milk to trust her with the baby any longer.

"You're pretty good at that for a beginner," Sam said. She held the other twin, a little girl.

"It's not so different than holding a puppy," Josh said.

"Speaking of puppies, have you seen what our dogs are doing right now?"

"No, what?" Josh asked, a feeling of dread in the pit of his stomach.

"Let's just say Layla's scarecrow will never have children of his own."

Josh grimaced. After Nikita was killed, Cam didn't have the heart to make Josh get rid of the puppies. So he had kept them all with the stipulation that they would all be fixed. Unfortunately with Sam's recovery and Layla's pregnancy, Josh had put off the procedure a little too long. Now there were three new sets of puppies creating havoc on the ranch, along with seven adult dogs who did nothing to try and keep order.

"Mom and Dad are here," Cade announced. He sounded tired. Neither he nor Layla had been getting much sleep the last couple of weeks since they brought the babies home from the hospital. Layla was napping now. The fact that she could sleep through all the family noise in the house was a testament to how exhausted she was. Sam had stayed home a couple of days to help out, but even with three people there was too much work.

The elder Kings entered the house and were introduced to their grandchildren with much fanfare and a few tears. Later that night after everything had settled down and supper had been eaten, Mrs. King made an announcement.

"Sam, I've finally finished your wedding portrait."

"Oh," Sam said. She felt the eyes of her sisters-in-law on her and tried not to laugh. "I can't wait to see what it looks like."

"None of us can," Belle added, all enthusiasm now as she gleefully rubbed her hands together in eager anticipation of the coming horror.

Mrs. King clapped her hands together excitedly as Josh slowly unwrapped the canvas. Sam stood back, waiting nervously. There was no mantel in their bedroom. Would they have to hang it in the living room?

Josh's image appeared first. His hair was an odd shade of orange, but otherwise he didn't look too bad. Then the canvas fell away and Sam was revealed. Everyone stood around in hushed silence.

"Mom, that's beautiful," Josh said, awed. Somehow his mother had captured Sam's vulnerable expression. Her big blue eyes were a perfect representation, and so were her porcelain complexion, heart-shaped face, and full lips.

"That looks *exactly* like her," Belle exclaimed, somewhat resentfully, Sam thought.

"How is that possible?" Ivy added in the same disbelieving tone.

"I closed my eyes and pictured how she looked when she picked up that gun and saved my son's life," Mrs. King said, casting a loving look at Sam.

Ivy and Belle glanced at each other.

"Did I mention I saved Coy's life when I made him wear his seatbelt?" Ivy said.

"And I pulled a lifeless Cam from the spring," Belle added.

Layla was in the nursery feeding the babies or she no doubt would have added her own amazing feat into the mix.

Mrs. King smiled happily. "Yes, I am truly blessed with my four wonderful daughters-in-law," she said. "Maybe I should do a painting of the four of you together."

Belle couldn't stop a small groan from escaping, but Sam didn't stick around to find out if Mrs. King heard her. She escaped into the bathroom where she collapsed onto the edge of the tub in a fit of convulsive laughter she could in no way contain. Not knowing why she suddenly darted from the room, Josh followed her to make sure she was okay. He smiled when he saw her face, blue eyes trained on him, overflowing with laughter and love. His heart felt the way it had every day for the past year, as if it were about to explode out of his chest with adoration. Silently he eased inside, locking the door behind him.

A while later when Coy went to use the bathroom, he realized someone was inside, or rather two someones. Doing a mental count of who was still in the living room, he froze in surprise that soon turned to amused approval. Laughing to himself, he turned and rejoined everyone in the living room. *Saint Josh, indeed.*

. . .

THANK you for reading *Cowboy Proud,* the fourth book in the Kings of Montana Series. For more books, please check out my website at www.vanessagraybartal.com

www.ingramcontent.com/pod-product-compliance
Lightning Source LLC
Chambersburg PA
CBHW021148190726
48288CB00008B/2883